DC
STREETS

Kevin Quattlebaum

Dedication

This book is dedicated to my mother Patricia Ann Quattlebaum, my brother Keith Quattlebaum, RIP, I love you both and I never stop missing you both. To Aunt Dean, Aunt Shirley, India, and the rest of the Quattlebaum, cousin Londoe and my man African Yummy. Thank you all for all the money, the pictures and all the encouraging words that was said while I was in here the belly of the beast. To my kids Lil Kevin, Kevin Myles, Lil Keith, Brianna, Patrice and Mya, daddy love you all and I can't wait to come home to be the father you all need. To my man geeking lover hood, from jersey, slim I couldn't have done it without you, you are one of the most well spoken word spitters I've ever met; if it wasn't for that chess no checker book you wrote I wouldn't have never finished this book. And the two I'm loving the two, don't think I forgot you Nina love you baby real recognize real thanks for everything.

Prologue

It was a rainy, gloomy night in Washington Hospital, which was in the heart of the mean streets of Washington DC. To the untrained eye, you'd be fooled by it being the Nation's Capital, but once you do an about face from the White House, there's more than what meets the eye. Pat was crying and screaming as she was in the process of giving births to her twin boys. The pain shot through her spine, then out the seams of her chest. She tried her hardest to follow the instructions of the chubby nurse.

"Breathe... Push....Breath...Push..." she coached her through what seemed to be the most painful experience of her life. When her first son was delivered, who she'd name Tim came out of her womb kicking and fighting, a smile creased her face but she knew the pain wasn't over; she had one more coming right behind him. Minutes later, she managed to push out another baby boy whom she named him Tony, but there seemed to be a problem, he wasn't moving.

What's wrong with my baby? Pat screamed demanding to know what was happening to her son. The doctor in charge had a smile on his face as he spoke, "Calm down, it's going to be alright". He cocked his hand back and smacked little Tony on his backside. Seeing him respond caused Pat to have a Kool-Aid smile on across her face.

Twenty Years Later

As the twins got older, they were on two separate paths in life. Tim was deep in the streets, already being knee deep in the drug game, making a name for himself in the DC streets. Tony on the other hand, was never involved in any type of illegal activity. He managed to work, play sports and maintain a 3.5 GPA at Howard University.

On this particular day Tony was on his way home from work. He was a Sales Representative at Hechinger Mall, which were a few blocks away from the home he shared with his mother. As he clocked out, he made his rounds, he prepared to head home for another night of studying, a hot shower, then have dinner with his mother. That was a typical day for Tony.

The sound of a car slamming on its brakes caused Tony to turn around, two masked men jumped out with pistols in hand.

"Lay your bitch ass on the ground!" One of the masked gunmen demanded. Tony did as he was told, hoping in the back of his mind that this would be over soon after they robbed him of the measly fifty seven bucks he had in his right pocket. His mind quickly changed once one of the gunmen kicked him in the ribs, causing him to curl up in pain. The other began to beat him across the back of his head with the butt of his pistol.

Tony felt the warm blood running down his face as he started to lose consciousness; he began to fade in and out.

Then the unthinkable happened.

Boom!....Boom!....Boom!....

One of the gunmen opened fire, hitting Tony three times in the back of the head.

The first bullet killed him; the other two just pushed his brain deeper out the front of what used to be his face.

The two masked men rushed back to their vehicle and sped off. Tony soaked in a puddle of his own blood, alone, another life taken on the mean DC Streets.

Chapter One

Knock...Knock...Knock!

"Who is it?" A female's voice called out from behind the door.

"It's MPD; can you please open the door ma'am?" One of the officers spoke; he was so used to these types of visits that it became second nature to him.

"What do you want? Go away!" The woman yelled, obviously not wanting to be bothered with by police.

"Ma'am, may we please speak with you? It's important that you open this door Ms. Gamble." He knew that saying her last name would get her attention.

Seconds later, the locks unlatched like he knew they would. It's a different story when you call someone's name out, but you know it's real when the police come to your door and say your name. Either someone died, or going to jail.

"What do you want?" The woman snapped. "And how did you know my name? I ain't done nothing. I paid them parking tickets weeks ago!" She tried to explain.

"Ma'am, may we come in please?" The shorter of the two officers asked.

She looked back and forth, seeing which one of her nosy neighbors was watching this unwanted encounter. "Hell no, you can't come in!" She shouted.

Becoming irritated, "Ma'am I'm Detective Stone and this is my partner Detective Brown. We're from the homicide task force. I'm so sorry to interrupt you, but we're here to inform you about a murder. Do you have a son named Tony Gamble?"

Pat was taken away, she lost her breath as she nodded her head and barely was able to say the words, "Yes, why do you ask?"

"Ma'am your son was found shot to death in the parking lot of Hechinger Mall at around 8:15p.m."

"If my son is dead, how the fuck do you know my address?" She asked with a look of suspicion.

"We found his identification on his persons with this address on it, now we're gonna need you to come to Washington Morgue to give us a positive identification of his body."

Pat lowered her head, trying hard to process what was being said, struggling with accepting the news she'd just received.

She raised her voice with every word she spoke, showing obvious emotion. Y'all want me to do what?! "Ma'am, please calm down." The officer said trying his best to calm the situation.

"Mah'fucker! You come in here telling me that my baby is dead! And you have the fucking nerve to tell me to calm down. Bitch, get the fuck out of my house, now!"

Both officers looked at each other knowing they'd seen this behavior numerous times before. With that being said they both turned around and headed for the door. As they exited the home, Pat slammed the door so hard that pictures fell off the walls. She stood there frozen, allowing the words she just heard to sink in.

****

Tim and his lil cousin lil Mike were riding around drinking Remy XO. Mike looked at the half empty bottle of Remy and shook his head.

"Damn Cuz," Mike slurred in his speech. "You damned near drank the whole bottle, mah'fucker we gotta make a pit stop."

"Aye Slim, shit don't feel right." Tim said totally ignoring Mike's comment to get more liquor. Just then at that very moment Tim's cell phone began to ring, he looked at his phone and noticed it was his mother's number. "Hello," he answered.

What he heard on the other end confirmed his suspicion, something was definitely wrong.

"Tim!" His mother's voice screamed through the speaker.

"Momma, what's wrong?"

"It's your brother! Tim....Tim....He....He gone!" She stuttered while she cried on the other end of the phone.

Tim was confused, "What! What you mean he gone?!"

Her crying got worst, "Some......body.....Somebody...Killed my baby!"

Tim's eyes instantly filled with tears, "Nah....Nah Mama," Tim moaned in grief. His heart had just been torn to pieces.

She tried to pull herself together for the sake of her other son, who'd just lost his twin brother. "Baby the police just left here, they took him to the Washington Morgue."

Tim couldn't believe the words he was hearing. Everything around him seems to stop. He wasn't focused on the road or anything else that was around him. The only thing that was on his mind was finding who killed his brother. Someone had to pay for this.

"Listen baby, I'm gonna need you to make sure it's him. You have to go to the morgue, I can't do it!"

"Are you gonna be alright till I get there?" He asked wanting to know if his mother was sane enough to be alone.

"Yea, I'll be ok till you get here. Please hurry, I need you son."

Tim hung up the phone, but his brain was in a daze, he couldn't focus.

"What's wrong cuz?" Mike asked seeing Tim's tears not knowing if the drink was fucking with him or not.

"Somebody killed Tony Slim," He said as he stared at Mike with tear filled eyes.

"Nah.....Nah Moe.....Not cuz!" Mike shouted as he tried to digest what he'd just heard. The rest of the ride to the morgue was in silence. Both men were having trouble coping with the news they just heard, they prayed it was a mistake.

When they finally reached Washington Morgue Tim quickly parked his car and rushed inside till they were met by a middle aged woman sitting at the desk.

"How may I help you?" She asked in a soft spoken voice, already knowing what they were there for.

"We're here to identify a body," Tim spoke up.

"What's the name?"

It hurt his heart to say his name, "Tony Gamble." Tim passed the lady a picture of Tony that he'd always kept in his wallet, she glanced at it briefly before she started pressing keys on her computer.

"Give me just a moment please," she spoke very soft somehow bringing a lot of comfort to this situation. After a minute or so, she looked up. "Ok, come with me." She led them into what they called the "Cold Room" where the bodies were kept. She looked at the chart then went to the number to where the body was stored. No matter how much he tried to prepare himself, Tim was not ready for what was next.

Once she pulled out the piece of slab, and then pulled back the sheet revealing Tony's body, everything moved in slow motion!

Tony's body was devastating!

His entire body was swollen and discolored. His face was mangled, dried up blood stained his lips. The worst part of all was the exit wounds of the bullet that ripped thru his skull. By the way his head was swollen; there were still bullets in his head.

Seeing his twin brother's body lying there on the gurney crushed every bit of Tim's soul.

He broke beyond his weakest state.

Unable to withstand it any further, he fell to the floor, landing on his knees. He placed his hands over his face and let out a scream. He stayed in that position until he was able to move again, his strength was gone.

Finally, he stood and kissed Tony on his forehead.

"I love you slim," he whispered as if Tony could hear him. He ran his hand thru his hair, as he did when they were kids years ago.

"He didn't deserve this," Mike said as he and Tim left out the City Morgue.

"Yeah, I know slim." Tim agreed. "Now, I have to let my mother know that her baby boy is never coming home again, this shit too real slim."

The ride from the City Morgue was a silent one; both men were in a state of shock, both men were in the mind frame of revenge!

Tim's heart was heavy, with the fact that he'd had to be the one responsible for telling his mother what he just saw.

The hope she was clinging onto was false.

Tony, was dead; and she was gonna have to accept the fact that her baby boy was never coming home again.

Momma! Tim yelled as he stepped into his mother's home.

When Pat saw the look on his face, mixed with the pain in his voice, her worst nightmare just had been confirmed.

Her son was dead.

"Oh my God nooooo! Tim, nooooo!" She cried out, she fell weak in her knees as Tim ran over to console her. She beat his chest, and began to convulse. She was in total distraught. Her son, the life she'd carried for nine months and gave birth too, had been stolen from her.

Seeing his mother cry the way she did caused Tim to breakdown. This was the second time in his life that he'd actually cried. The first time was just minutes ago when he'd laid eyes on the dead body of his lil brother.

Seven Days Later

The Funeral

Tony's funeral was held at Stewart's Funeral Home located on Bennett Road. From all the Bentley's, Benz's and tricked out SUV's parked outside the funeral home, it was pretty much obvious what kind of lifestyles the people in attendance lived. Everyone of status came to pay their respects to the late Tony Gamble, and show love and support for Tim and his family.

Reverend Stephen Wood presided over the lovely, well planned service. When it came to his brother's home-going, Tim spared no expenses. The casket was cream colored and made of titanium. He was dressed in a white Gucci suit, accompanied by a blue Gucci shirt.

Even in his coffin, he was one of the flyest in the room.

There were enough flowers in the funeral parlor to start a Botanical Garden.

Tim and his fiancé "Niecy" sat next to his mother and the rest of the immediate family. As the funeral was nearing a close, Rev. Wood asked that everyone in attendance stand while the family headed toward the awaiting limos. Once everyone was in their respective cars, and the casket had been loaded into the hearse, the Procession to the cemetery began.

After the funeral, the family went to Trinidad Baptist Church for the repast.

Tim held back wanting to say his final farewell, but remained to stay dry-eyed through the entire service.

He wanted to remain strong for his mother.

I can't believe this shit, Tim thought while looking at the spot his brother had been laid to rest, and then it happened. All the tears he'd been trying to withhold fell from his eyes.

"I love you, slim," Tim whispered as he fell to his knees beside his brother's gravesite. "I know God doesn't make mistakes, so I guess this is all part of the plan. But I'll tell you this much; if it takes me the rest of my life, I'm gon kill that mah'fucka that did this to you. That's on everything I love."

Tim wiped his eyes then stood to his feet. He looked over at his right hand man "Tec" who'd stayed behind with him for support.

"Tec, I need you slim. We gotta find out who killed my brother slim," Tim said with pain in his voice meaning every word he said. "I don't care what we do, if I gotta shoot this whole fucking city up! We gotta find who da fuck did this shit!

In Tim's mind, everyone was a suspect. If a nigga even appeared to be doing anything out of pocket, they were potential targets!

The word was out, and everyone in the hood knew Tim had a twenty thousand dollar reward out for anyone with information regarding the dead man walking responsible for pulling the trigger. In a matter of days the ghetto internet said that the SUV seen fleeing the scene of the crime belonged to a nigga named "Duke." Duke and his bamma ass brother "Darrell" were known stick up kids throughout the city and Tim got word instantly.

While on the way to his mother's house Tim's cell phone vibrated on his thigh, he looked at the caller id to see who the call was coming from before answering it.

It was his pat'nah "Big Jack."

"What's good Jo?" Tim asked as he answered his phone.

"T, where you at?"

"I just pulled up around my way, why what's up?" Tim asked eager to get to the point of the phone call.

"Slim, I need to holla at chu ASAP! You gon' love this."

"Say no more. Just tell me when and where."

"Meet me at Eddie Leonard's Pizza Shop."

"I'm on my way."

Tim and Jack were good friends with a solid mutual love for one another. Although they were from different parts of town, real recognize real, so the bullshit never came between them. So Tim knew that whatever Jack had for him was gonna be worth the trouble.

He hit the gas and sped over to the pizza spot.

As he pulled into the parking lot he noticed Jack standing by his Q45 Infinity, he swiftly pulled up next to him and Jack entered the vehicle.

"What's up slim?" Jack said as he and Tim embraced.

After a brief conversation, Jack hopped out and he and Tim parted ways.

Later That Night

Tec and Mike sat in a tinted out, black F-150 pickup truck. They were focused on a home about twenty feet away from where they were parked. It was 2:31am when Duke's truck pulled into the driveway of the home they were watching.

Duke put his truck in park, staggering from a few drinks he'd had about an hour before. As he exited the SUV, then hit the alarm, he approached his home while fumbling with his keys. As he went to put the key into the lock, he heard a noise behind him.

It was too late!

In a desperate attempt he reached for his weapon, but the feeling of cold steel pressed against the back of his head told him not to.

        "Bitch, I wish you would." Tec said thru clenched teeth. His Ruger 45 was locked and loaded on Duke's head, and one false move it would be over. With his free hand Tec relieved Duke of his weapon.

Mike took Duke's house keys, then opened the front door to the home. Duke was forced in and ordered to get on his knees. Mike checked the house to make sure no one else was inside.

"Why....Why are you... doing this to me?" Duke pleaded. I've never done anything to...to you." He continued to stutter. "I don't even know you."

"Shut the fuck up, before I kill yo bitch ass!" Mike yelled as he came back to the front room.

Mike was a fierce man, in his mid-twenties with eyes of an experienced killer.

Crack!

He slapped Duke upside the head with the butt of his 357 crossover, blood gushed from his head. Feeling no remorse, he continued to pistol whip Duke until he was curled up in a fetal position and crying like a bitch. Tec had to pull Mike off of him.

He would have killed Duke, if he didn't!

Tim's eyes were bloodshot red as he sat in a rental car awaiting the phone call. Gun in hand, and finger on the trigger. The phone finally rang.

"Hello," he answered.

The person on the other end spoke briefly.

"Bet!" Tim said with a look of hatred in his eyes.

Then minutes later Tim was pulling up behind the stolen F-150. He checked his pistol, then took it off safety. He looked around, then casually walked into Duke's house.

Duke, on the other hand was hog tied in the middle of his living room, with a strip of duct tape around his mouth. It was clear that Duke had been beaten, from the obvious bumps, lumps, and blood gushing from the side of his head.

He was pretty fucked up!

Tim and Duke made stern eye contact as he screwed the Wilson Suppressor on his Smith & Wesson 38, He knelt beside Duke before he spoke, "nigga, I'm gonna take off this duct tape and give you one chance to tell me who killed my brother." He then snatched off the duct tape.

Duke's mind began to wonder, he thought about his last few bodies. He knew exactly who Tim was, but he still tried to lie. "I....I...don't...."

Bow!

Tim smacked him upside his head with the butt of his gun. The force of the blow opened yet another gash on Duke's head. He looked up, staggering to register his whereabouts.

Tim was tired of waiting.

Boc!...Boc!...Boc!...Boc!....Boc!....Boc!...

Tim choked the trigger six times, releasing every bullet he had into Duke's head. His lifeless body lay slumped in a circular pool of his own blood and brain matter.

Tec, and Mike left to finish phase two of their mission while Tim made his way home. He was doing 75 mph on the beltway when his mind was flooded with thoughts of his lil brother Tony. There wasn't a day since his murder that he hadn't thought about him, and today was no different.

When he pulled his car into the driveway and parked next to Niecey's X5 BMW. He sat in the car listening to the engine for a few minutes still in deep thought about his brother. He was struggling with the fact that he has to accept the fact that he would never see his twin brother again. He flashed back to the last birthday they shared together.

"Aye, Tim I wanna tap that pussy right there." He told his brother while staring at one of the models that were selected to serve drinks at their party.

"That's what you want slim?" Tim knew his brother had no problems with the ladies, he was just a bit shy when it came to bad bitches, and she was one of them.

After five minutes of negotiating, Tony left early with the chocolate stallion on his arm. "Thanks bruh." He could hear Tony saying over and over in his head.

That was a day he'd never forget as long as he lived.

Grabbing the gun off the armrest he made his way inside the house. After unlocking all four of the special locks he'd had installed, he quickly ran over to the ADT system to disarm the alarm before it woke up Niecy. He tiptoed upstairs then entered the bedroom. Niecy was laying in the bed curled up half asleep.

She could never fully sleep when she didn't have her man in the bed with her. And somehow she always had this sixth sense when she knew he was up to something.

Tim smiled as he peeled off his clothes then made his way to bed. He eased in behind Niecy, taking her into his arms, and planting small kisses on her back. She lay with a smile on her face knowing her man was home, and most important he was safe!

Tim slid his hand gently down to Niecy's freshly shaved pussy, this caused her to moan and bite her bottom lip. He continued to remove the wife beater she wore, and then played with her nipples the way he knew she liked it.

Once she was naked, she helped him out of his polo boxer briefs. She stared him deep into his eyes as she took his dick into her mouth slowly. She took him whole into her mouth, she watched his facial expressions which only made her more aggressive. Tim moaned and groaned as she worked her head back and forth, then up and down with a mouth full of spit. Niecy's head game was on one thousand and she knew it, and right now the way she had Tim's toes curling was no different.

When she nearly drove him to climax, she came up for air and Tim took control of the situation before him. He flipped her over then quickly entered her missionary style. He loved her fuck faces, the way she would suck her own titties drove him crazy every time. They went at it like this for hours before finally falling asleep.

****

Tim was still asleep, drained from the good sex he'd just had. When Niecy exited the bathroom wearing nothing but a wife beater, she couldn't help but look at herself in the full length mirror that hung in their bedroom.

Damn, I look good. She thought as she looked at her own ass. The hourglass shape she had, with a perky pair of 34C cup titties, and a round 40" ass.

She looked down and stared at her fresh Mani/Pedi. Tim had a lust about her feet, and how she looked in a pair of open toe stiletto heels. The fastest way to start an argument with Tim was simple. If she didn't keep her fingernails and feet done, she knew it would be hell to pay.

After lusting off herself, she began to pick Tim's clothes off the floor. She did a double take and noticed what seemed to be blood on their brand new Persian rug. A million and one thoughts crossed her mind, but she didn't stress it any further. Instead, she went into the bathroom to get a rag and some cold water to clean the stain from the carpet.

When she was done, she got rid of the rag and climbed in the bed beside her man. She was a good woman, a submissive woman and she would approach the situation in due time.

Two Hours Later

Tim was awakened by the sound of someone crying. When he looked over he noticed Niecy sitting up in the bed next to him with a face full of tears. She was staring at the television. He followed her eyes to see what was it that had her so distraught.

It was breaking news on channel seven.

"This is Rhonda Bruce and I'm reporting live for NBC news, Here I am in the Trinidad area where Donald "Duke" Miller was found brutally beaten and shot to death execution style. Sources close to the investigation say that Miller was a suspect in the slaying of a DC man who was murdered while leaving work in the Hechinger Mall parking lot just a week or so ago. Is this retaliation? Or another murder on our DC Streets? We'll keep you updated as more information becomes available. Back to you Jean."

On the Other Side of Town

Darrell was laid up with his baby mother Dominique when his phone began ringing constantly. He wanted to ignore the call, but something inside told him otherwise.

"Hello," he answered on the third ring.

"Darrell!" His sister Ebony screamed through the receiver.

Instantly, he knew something was wrong. "What's going on?"

"Darrell....Somebo....Somebody...Kil....Killed ...Duke! The cops....Just....Just.....found his body this morning!" she cried as she tried to get the words out.

"Fuck!"

After hearing his sister explain what she knew so far, his body went numb. He felt as if someone stabbed him in his heart. He hung up with his sister then jumped out the bed in search of his clothes. He was in such a rush he put on his jeans with no underwear.

Dominique knew something was wrong, "baby, what's wrong?"

He ignored her and opened his drawer, then pulled out a pistol.

"Baby what's wrong!?" she repeated, not liking the fact that he ignored her.

He looked up at her with a look of sadness, "Duke's dead," he muttered.

"What….What the fuck happened?" she said with a look of confusion.

After checking to make sure he'd had a full clip, Darrell headed for the door.

"Darrell, please don't go out there. Baby please listen to me!" She literally begged him to stay knowing whatever his brother was involved in would eventually find him. Tears began to well in her eyes, she knew nothing positive would come from this. In an attempt to keep him in the house she grabbed him. They shared a passionate kiss, but his mind was set.

He was going to find out who killed his brother, and put some work in!

Tec and Mike sat outside of Darrell's house in a stolen F-150. Tec was staring out the window while Mike was reloading his 357 Crossover with hollow points.

"Tec, this nigga better bring his bamma ass out'chere be'fo I go up in there. I'll kill him, and that pretty ass bitch." He laughed, "Shit if the kid old enough I'll put two in his lil ass too." He said joking, but meaning every word.

Some people don't have the ability to conceal their feelings. They become open books, saying whatever comes to mind.

Mike was one of those people.

A few minutes later, Darrell came out the house, briskly walking to his S80 Volvo. Mike pulled his hoodie over his head, then hopped out the pickup with his 357 in hand. Darrell was attempting to open the door to his car when shots started to rang out.

Boom....Boom....Boom....Boom....Boom ....Boom....!

Mike fired all six shots, thus dropping Darrell like a bad habit. Seeing his work was done, Mike ran back to the pickup truck, and he and Tec sped off.

****

Tim was on his way to see his mother when his phone rang. It was his natural habit to check the caller ID before answering.

"Yeah," he answered.

"Done," the voice on the other end said.

"Cool," Tim replied before hanging up with a smile on his face.

He'd never doubted that his boys would accomplish their mission. He just didn't want Mike to go overboard, which he was known to do at times. He had a legendary temper, and was known for employing overkill.

It don't even matter, job well done!

Chapter 2

Detective Stone was sitting at his desk sipping on a Starbuck's coffee when he got the call about the murder of 21st and I street. He was slightly frustrated because he was still tied up with the murder of the deceased Donald "Duke" Miller, and now less than twenty four hours later he's had another one on his hands. He picked up the phone from his messy desk and called his partner Mike Brown.

"Hey, Stone's. What's up?" Det. Brown asked from the other end of the phone. "Mike, we have another body," he informed his partner. "Check this out, Donald Miller's brother Darrell, was found shot to death on 21st, just moments ago. I'm on my way to the crime scene now."

"Alright, I'll meet you there."

Homicide Detective, Mike Brown sighed in frustration. He was on his way to follow up a lead that he'd gotten from one of his confidential informants concerning the Gamble murder. "I guess that will have to wait," he mumbled to himself as he changed directions and headed toward 21st and I street.

****

Det. Stone arrived at the scene almost fifteen minutes later. By this time a large crowd of onlookers had surrounded the scene. Brown was standing near the black body bag. "Wanna take a look?"

Once the body bag was unzipped, Darrell's face was swollen and covered in dried up blood. He had a hole the size of a nickel in his forehead, however the exit wound took out a chunk of his skull. To the Detective's trained eyes, it was obvious that he'd been hit with a high caliber weapon.

While Brown studied the crowd with a detached concentration, Stone quietly surveyed the surrounding area. He was turning to speak to a patrol officer when Dominique burst out the house crying and screaming.

She was clearly devastated.

In one full stroke, she'd lost her soulmate, best friend, and child's father.

Det. Stone let her cry for a minute before going over to speak to her.

After Darrell's body was loaded onto a gurney, and taken to the awaiting coroner van, Det. Brown approached a group of bystanders. He asked if any of them had seen anything, but no one answered. Instead, he was met with a wary silence of people who didn't care to speak to police. In the mean streets of DC of course you had your snitches, but no one would dare do it out in the open and live to talk about it later.

And they knew it!

******

Ever since the death of his brother, Tim had shut down all his drug spots. All business had to be put on hold. He ran a building on L Street called the "Carter." The name came from the infamous movie New Jack City, but this was the real thing. This Carter was known for having the best coke, all day every day, twenty-four hours, and seven days a week. A fiend could come with nothing, and upon purchase could cop a stem pipe, a place to get high, and have another fiend to get high with.

But today, it was a ghost town.

As Tim entered the Carter, he was greeted by his partners Shawn new recruit, Rick. He was standing guard, armed with a Heckler and Koch MP5 with an extended banana clip, which held 80 rounds.

"What's up Slim?" Rick asked, trying to break the tension and make small talk. Tim simply responded with a head nod. As he entered the room he saw that Shawn and Dat were sitting at the table drinking and chit-chattin.

"It's about time mah'fucker," Shawn said with a smile on his face.

Shawn was a money-gettin nigga, he had a block that sold just as much coke as the Carter. His money was long, but his only problem was he couldn't keep a solid connect. He had a bad habit on trickin off his money on bitches, and clothes. And in this game, your mind has to be in the right place, or the money will go just as fast as it came.

Now Dat, he was from the south side. He hung out in Potomac Garden. A rough project known for murders, and heavy drug traffic. People called him Dat because he stuttered, but nevertheless, he was a fly nigga as well. Regardless to what time of day you saw him, he stayed draped in the latest fashion, pushing a fly whip, and riding with a bad bitch. He loved to talk that "Big Willie Shit".

"What's up men?" Tim greeted them, then got right down to business. First and foremost I want to apologize to y'all on the money tip. Both of y'all know that I've been going through some shit, but shits about to get back to normal. So I' ma need y'all niggas to get ready.

"Read...Ready...Ready?" Dat interjected. "I...I...I Been Ready."

The men shared a laugh, then for the next twenty minutes they got down to business. Tim's hiatus had seriously hampered their cash flow. Now, things were on its way to getting back to normal.

After handling his business at the Carter, Tim headed home. He called Niecy to remind her to pick up their dinner from Ruth Chris Steakhouse. On the way home he realized that since his brother's death he hadn't been spending quality time with her. He'd managed to let the urge for revenge cause problems in his household, and even though Tim was no stranger to the streets, and how things went. He also knew that home front had to be taken care of. So now that the situation had been dealt with, he could get things back right with his woman.

Tim was so into thinking about Niecy and his plans on marrying her soon, that he'd lost focus for a second. He looked in his rearview and noticed a white Crown Victoria riding his bumper. "Here we go," he mumbled to himself as he switched lanes and sped up. The Crown Victoria changed lanes as well and continued to follow at a close distance. Tim was able to get a view of the plates, "MPD…..What the fuck is this bamma ass shit," Tim hissed as he approached a stop light. He banged a right then pulled into the Amoco gas station. He sat in his car scanning the entire area for the Crown Vic, but it was nowhere to be found. Finally, Tim pulled off and headed home in Accokeek, Maryland.

*****

Four vans full of law enforcement officials dressed in riot gear and carrying assault rifles pulled up in front of an estate in Upper Marlboro, Maryland. The head officer hopped out first and led the way with the rest of his team bringing up the rear.

Inside, Rome had his longtime lover Trina bent over on all fours. Sounds of love making could be heard throughout the entire house. Trina was soaking wet as Rome pulled her hair and choked her slightly, He was pumping in and out of her like a crazed dog, then suddenly he pulled out.

"No, no baby," Trina moaned softly. I'm about to cum.

Ignoring her pleas, Rome spun her around to face him. He then parted her thighs, and spread her lower pair of lips. He dove his tongue in her pussy as if it were his last supper. She used both hands to push him inside her pussy, thrusting her hips into his face. She was on the verge of cumming as he flicked his tongue in and out her sweet tasting pussy.

Rome felt her legs trembling and he knew she was to the point of ecstasy when he heard.

"Freeze!, put your hands in the air where I can see them!" The police yelled as they entered the room.

Rome and Trina found themselves naked and covered in each other's sweat with seven AR15 Rifles pointed at them.

Needless to say, Trina never got her nut off!

*****

Tim and Niecy had finished their dinner; they sipped on a bottle of Cristal while sitting in front of their seventy-two inch plasma television flipping through channels. Tim stopped at the Channel Seven News flash that grabbed his attention.

"This is Rhonda Bruce from Channel 7 Eyewitness News. Today a Maryland man by the name of Rome Jones has been taken into Federal custody. The ATF and the FBI were both present during the arrest. Jones is being accused of transporting massive amounts of cocaine between Atlanta and the DMV region. The US Attorney is charging Jones with being head of this criminal enterprise. If found guilty, Jones face a life sentence in federal prison. He is also being charged with conspiracy to possess cocaine with the intent to distribute. At the time of the arrest Jones 3.5 million dollar estate was surrounded and searched. The agents confiscated two million dollars in cash, a 2010 Lamborghini, a 2010 Phantom Rolls Royce, and a 2011 Maserati.

Jones is currently being held in an Upper Marlboro detention center. We will bring you more details as this story unfolds. This is Rhonda Bruce, reporting live for channel Seven news.

Tim slammed his fist into the coffee table, he couldn't believe his eyes or his ears. He immediately dialed Trina's number, but it went straight to voicemail. He knew that she was most likely somewhere being questioned.

Tim had left the house and was on his way to meet Tec when his cell phone started ringing. He saw Trina's number and quickly answered.

"Hello"

"Tim, the po…"

Not intending to be rude, he cut her off. He knew just how reckless women could be on the phones, and he didn't want to take any chances.

"Look Trina, just meet me at the same spot where Slim used to meet me at. We can talk when you get there."

"Alright, I'll be there in thirty minutes." She said before hanging up the phone.

Thirty Minutes Later

Tim was nodding his head and singing along to Akon's and Stylez P song "Locked Up". He couldn't help but think about Rome's situation. He pulled into the parking lot in front of a flower shop and killed the ignition. He reached for his pistol and sat it on his lap as he waited for Trina to show up.

"Where she at?" Tim wondered as he looked at his watch. She was fifteen minutes late. Growing frustrated he was about to call her phone when her 650 BMW pulled into the parking lot. She pulled up next to Tim's car and hopped out. As she approached, Tim could see the pain and hurt written all over her face. He couldn't help but to feel sorry for her.

"Hey sis," Tim greeted her as she got in the car with him. "What happened?"

Tears fell from her eyes as she spoke. The fucking feds kicked our door in, they fucked our house up Tim! They took him!

"Did they have a warrant?"

"They had some papers in their hands, I don't know if it was or not. I was scared to death. I don't know what to do."

"Did you call the lawyer?"

"Yea, I called Mr. Tutt and he said he'll go see Rome. He's gonna call me as soon as he finds something. I'm so confused and lost right now, that's why I called you Tim."

"Trina, it's gonna be alright. Trust me, he gave her some comforting words. If you want, you can stay with me and Niecy for as long as you need too."

"Thanks Tim, I'm gonna have my brother come stay with me and help me clean that mess up. I have to find out what Rome wants me to do."

"Do you need any money? Anything, you know I got you."

"Nah, I'm good. You know Rome kept something to the side just in case. My baby always two steps ahead of the game."

"Trina, if you need anything. No matter what it is, you call me, no matter what time it is, ok?"

"I will, and as soon as the lawyer calls and tells me what's up, I'll hit you as well."

"Cool," Tim said as he and Trina embraced,

As she made her way out the car Tim stepped out behind her. He wanted to ask her if she'd been followed but he figured now wasn't a good time, she'd been through enough for one day.

She looked back at him, her eyes were glossy from the tears she was holding back. The mere sight of Tim made her think about Rome. She hugged him once more, and Tim could feel her pain. He knew she was trying to hold it together, but the pain was too deep. No matter what, he'd do what he had to for Trina, she was family, and family looked out for one another. In good and bad times.

Chapter 3

Rome's initial hearing was scheduled for 9:30 am. Trina set her alarm for 6:30am she wanted to get an early start so she could be the first person to enter the courtroom. And she was. She made sure she was looking good for her man. She wore a Gucci dress, coupled with a pair of six inch matching Gucci stilettos. Her makeup was flawless, and her jewelry was shining. She was proud to be Rome's woman, and she wanted it seen in her appearance. When the Marshals brought Rome from the back of the courtroom he was wearing an orange jumpsuit, which made him look more like a criminal. When he locked eyes with Trina his eyes opened wide and a smile creased his cheeks. Together they were glowing from seeing one another.

Rome took a seat next to his lawyer. Harry Tutt was a small man in size, but he was well respected, even feared by some of the best prosecutors in his district. He was known as the best trial lawyer in town.

"All rise." The bailiff ordered as the judge emerged his chamber. "Your honor, we have docket number 05-235, the United States of America versus Mr. Rome Jones. In charge of the prosecution is District Attorney Mr. Jeffrey

Pealman, and Mr. Harry Tutt representing the defendant.

"Good morning!" Judge Bates greeted the courtroom as he looked over the stack of paper sitting in front of him. "Counsel, are we prepared to move forward this morning?"

"The government is ready!" Mr. Pealman responded.

"And you, Mr. Tutt?

"Yes, your honor, the defense is ready as well." Mr. Tutt spoke clearly..

"Nice bow tie, Mr. Tutt!" The Judge complimented.

"Thank you, it's a gift from the wife."

Rome's instincts kicked in, hearing the friendly bond between his lawyer and the judge, he was sure that he would be granted a bail.

The judge cleared his throat before he spoke, "Do to the seriousness of these charges, I am denying bail at this time Mr., Jones, I am reprimanding you into custody of the Marshal's department.

Rome looked back at Trina, then blew her a kiss. Then he put his hand by his ear making an I'll call you gesture. Trina understood. She blew him a kiss back, and then nodded her head letting him know that she'd be awaiting his call.

As the Marshal's led Rome out the courtroom, Harry Tutt began gathering his papers. Trina left the courtroom shortly after Rome was out of sight. When Harry finally exited he found Trina sitting in the waiting area.

"Mrs. Jones, how are you doing?" He spoke to her.

"I'm fine, considering the situation."

"Please call me Harry." He told her before he continued. "As you heard, I'm sure. Your husband was denied bond, but I've already filed a motion for a bond hearing next Tuesday."

Trina felt slightly relieved, she wanted her husband home with her by all cost. "Do you think the judge will grant bail?" She asked.

"I'm not one hundred percent sure, but he did say "at this time" so I'll do my best to convince him."

"Thank you so much, Harry."

"I'm just doing my job, Rome is a good guy." He said with a smile on his face. "It was nice meeting you Mrs. Jones. I'll keep in touch, but for now, just relax and try to get some rest." He said as they shook hands and parted ways.

As soon as Harry walked off, Trina pulled out her phone to call Tim.

"Hey Trina, he answered. What's up?"

Rome went to court this morning, she said into the phone. They kept him, but his lawyer already put in for another hearing next week.

Tim let out a deep breath. "Ok, you alright Trina?"

"Yea I'm cool. I just want my man home that's all, I miss him already."

"I know....I know... It will be alright."

"Alright, Tim I'll hit chu later. I'm going to get something to eat."

"Aight, call me later."

After hanging up with Trina, Tim sat back and thought about the conversation he'd had with Rome earlier. He knew what had to be done. Logging on to his computer, he went to a travel site and booked a flight and hotel room.

The Next Day

The next morning, Tim and Tec were boarding a direct flight from BWI (first class) to Atlanta. Tim looked over at Tec knowing how he felt uneasy about flying. With a smirk on his face he asked, what's up Tec? You good?

Come on with the bullshit Slim, Tec nervously responded. You fucking know how I feel about flying.

Let me find out, Tim laughed at him again. Ol'bamma ass nigga scared of flying.

Nigga you think you funny. Let's see if you still think it's funny if one of these Bin Laden mah'fuckers got a bomb strapped to their chest.

Tec, looked at Tim and noticed his mind was elsewhere. "You aight playboy?"

"Yea, I'm cool, just thinking about Rome that's all."

Rome was Tim's connect, but they'd been friends long before that. There was no doubt in his mind what he needed to do, and he also knew in his heart that Rome would have done the same for him, if the shoe was on the other foot.

After landing at the Hartsfield Jackson Int'l Airport, Tec and Tim got off the plane and headed to the baggage area. Tec was listening to his iPod, nodding his head to the latest backyard band song while Tim pulled out his phone to make a call.

"What's up Tim?" The voice on the other end of the phone answered.

"Shit, waiting on you slim. Where you at?"

"I'm out front."

"Cool, I'll be out in a second, let me grab my bags."

Mal was Pat's sister Dean son, which made him and Tim first cousins. Mal left DC to visit Atlanta six years ago and never returned.

After grabbing their luggage, Tim and Tec made their way to the entrance to find Mal sitting on the hood of a cocaine white Range Rover. He was draped in Prada, big boy shades and enough jewelry to front a music video.

Nigga, bring ya ass on! Mal yelled exposing a mouthful of diamonds.

Tim tapped Tec on the shoulder, look at this bamma nigga down here flossin, Tim smiled. If I knew he was gonna be pulling up like one of them BMF niggas, I would've caught a cab.

"Wat up cousin?" Mal asked in a strong country accent.

"What's up Big Meech?" Tim joked again.

Mal's body language shifted, "Aye, go head with that Big Meech shit, he looked at Tec. You still hanging with this hating ass nigga?"

Tec couldn't hold his laughter, "Yea that's my man Slim."

After putting their bags in the trunk, Mal made his way through traffic with ease. Making it known these were his streets now. Tim, was about to put in a Rick Ross cd when Mal looked at him and said, "I wish you would. Tim sat back while Mal kept talking. Nigga fall da fuck back and keep your hands to yourself, he snapped. There's only one DJ in this mah'fuckin ride."

"My bad, Big Meech," Tim said while holding his hands up in a mock surrender.

Mal seemed slightly irritated by that statement.

"Nigga, I told you about that Big Meech shit!"

They spent the rest of the ride laughing and joking. When they reached the hotel people stood around trying to see who was gonna get out of the chromed out Range Rover on twenty four inch rims. All the attention had Tim's stomach doing flips. Mal turned down his Bose sixteen speaker sound system then extended his hand for a pound, showing off his Breitling wristwatch.

"I'll hit chu when I'm on my way back," he said.

"Aight cousin. Be safe."

"Nigga, I'm always good, Mal said lifting his armrest to let Tim see the desert eagle 44 he packing."

When Tim exited the Range Rover and saw the way people were gawking at him, instantly took him back to Rome and his current situation with the feds.

"You aight Slim?" Tec asked noticing the change in his mood.

Tim shook it off.

"Yea, I was just thinking bout Rome's situation again," Tim responded.

Tec spoke from the heart, "Slim, don't even sweat that shit. We gon do what we came down here to do, and all is gonna work out. Trust me."

"Ain't no question!"

They made their way to the front of the hotel, the doorman showed them to the front desk. The receptionist was rather cute. She was brown skin, nice shape with a small mole on her face.

"Welcome to the Marriott, she smiled. How can I help you? "She caught them getting out of the expensive vehicle, so she figured they were drug dealers or athletes.

"We have reservations, Tim said passing her his ID and credit card." She took the information and punched his name on the computer.

"So how are you doing today, Robin?" Tim asked smiling like they were old friends. She smiled back, wondering how he knew her name. She was so lost in the moment that she'd forgotten she wore a name tag. She secretly checked Tim out as she finished his paperwork for his room. When she was done, she had Tim sign, then passed his documents back to him, but not before brushing her hand against his.

"Thank you for choosing the Marriott, Mr. Gamble. Enjoy your stay."

"I will, hopefully I'll enjoy you before I leave," he flashed a smile then grabbed his key cards.

When they entered the room, Tim was ready to take a shower. Before he could take his clothes off his phone began to vibrate. Telling him he has a text message. He picked up his phone and seen that the message was from Mal.

It read: **From: Cousin**

Yo cuz! I should be there in an hour. Everything's a go. Peace.

Time Sent 1:28 pm

"What's up Tim?" Tec asked as he flipped through the channels on the oversized television.

"That was Mal, he said he should be here in an hour."

Knowing time was limited, he hopped in the shower to get himself mentally ready for what he was about to do. There was no compassion in his heart when it came to rats!

He would show no mercy.

One Hour Later

When Tim and Tec made their way out the hotel, Mal was outside awaiting them. A white female with a body like Ice T's wife Coco exited the driver's side of the black Malibu that was parked behind Mal's Range Rover. She strutted her way to the passenger side of Mal's SUV. Mal rubbed his hands together and smiled while passing Tim the keys.

"Here you go," he looked at him with a look of concern.

"I see you fuckin with them snow bunnies," Tim said thinking about the lips and hips on the girl in Mal's truck.

"Ah shit, here we go with this hating ass shit again," Mal laughed it off. "I don't care if a bitch was green, she bad. I'm hitting it!"

"Ain't no secret!" Tec agreed.

Mal changed the subject, "Aye, everything you asked for is in the trunk. Tec reached in the backseat and pulled down the console leading to the trunk. There was a Versace duffle bag sitting there. Tec grabbed it, sat it on his lap and unzipped it. He pulled out a P89 Ruger, and a Glock Subcompact 45. Tec smiled at the sight of the Ruger, which was his favorite handgun of all.

"K, you know I need this Ruger. You take the fo'pound," he suggested.

"Do you, Slim." Knowing Tec had a fetish for guns.

They drove in silence until they reached a parking lot way out in the Bankhead area. "Do you see what I see?" Tim asked pointing at the Bentley Coupe with the Maryland tags.

Tec nodded with a sinister smile on his face. Both men cocked their pistols, making sure they had full clips and the safeties were off! They were about to exit the car till a young lady walked out of one of the shops that sat in the lot. Tec raised his pistol to fire, but Tim stopped him.

"Hold fast Slim," Tim held him back.

The young lady got into a white Audi A8 and drove off. Seconds later, Putt walked out of the same shop the young lady came from.

"I'm on his ass!" Tec said as he made his move.

Putt, was on his cellphone with a smile on his face obviously having a good conversation when Tec ran down on him firing shots from his Ruger.

Boc....Boc....Boc...Boc...Boc!

Putt was hit in the torso and neck which knocked him off his feet. His breath became short, and his chest tightened. He had no idea where the shots came from, or who was shooting. He'd thought he was caught up in a drive by of some sort. Just when he thought he wasn't the intended target, he looked up and locked eyes with none other than Tim. He had a Glock 45 at his side.

Oh shit, he thought as Tim aimed the gun at his head.

"This is for Rome you rat ass bitch!" Tim yelled before squeezing the trigger putting five bullets in Putt's head.

He was dead before Tim stopped firing.

Tec looked around, "K, come on slim. Let's get the fuck outta here!"

Together, they took off running back to the Malibu, and peeled off. After driving a few blocks, Tim pulled over on the side of the warehouse. After wiping off both guns, Tec hopped out and tossed them both into the sewer. When he got back in the car, Tim was smiling as he reminisced on the day he first took a liking to Tec...

******

One evening while walking home from the local rec center Tec decided to take a shortcut through an alley on Maryland Avenue. As he was walking down the alley he saw Tim standing over a man firing his pistol. Tec dove to the ground in fear of Tim seeing him. When Tec finally looked up, Tim was gone and the man was dead on the ground in a pool of his own blood. Tec took off running and made his way home. He was glad that he'd made it safely until he saw Tim standing on his apartment stairs.

"What's up Tec?" Tim greeted him with an unreadable face. "Look, I know what you saw back there. I'm gonna need you to keep that between me and you."

"You ain't gotta worry about me," Tec said noticing how careful Tim was observing him. "I can't stand a snitch! My brother doing life because of a hot ass nigga." Tim reached in his pocket and pulled out a large stack of bills, but Tec waved him off. "Nah, slim. Keep your money."

Tim was shocked, and confused that he refused to take the money. It was obvious that he and Tec shared the same morals and principles.

Tec noticed the smile appear on Tim's face, "What?" Tec asked wondering what the hell he was smiling about.

"Nigga, I love you." Tim said. "You know, you and Mike are like brothers to me."

With that being said, he snapped outta his trance and headed back toward the hotel.

Chapter 4

One Week Later

Tim pulled up in front of Bubble's barber shop. Bubble was an ol'head in his early sixties. In his younger days, Bubble was one of the biggest drug dealers in New York. After some of his close associates got arrested and started snitching, Bubble packed up and moved his family to DC. Being smart and knowing the feds can come at any time, he put his money into a barber shop and a few other things. He'd been living comfortable ever since.

Nina, Bubble's wife was coming out the barber shop wearing a juicy velour sweat suit, which made her ass look phatter than what it was. Nina was in her early thirties, standing 5'4, with a pretty round pie shaped face and thick lips.

She was a bad bitch! And you couldn't tell her she wasn't the shit.

She'd never imagined herself cheating on Bubble, but it was something about Tim that drove her crazy.

She knew she had to have him.

The way she saw it, his swagger was turn't up, and the streets respected him.

That mixed with his good looks and the rumors she heard about him in the bedroom just pulled her in like a magnet.

As Tim was getting out of his car, Nina put an extra pep in her step as she approached him. "When you gonna give me a ride in that nice car?" She asked with lustful eyes.

"Come on Nina," Tim peeped game. "You know Mr. Bubble wouldn't like that. You not bout to have your father kill me." Tim said trying to see just how far she would go.

She smiled, showing a set of pearly whites. "I see you got jokes." she started to laugh a bit, "You know damn well Bubble ain't my father."

Putting his hands up in surrender, "My bad," Tim matched her laugh. "Nina, you take care of yourself." He dismissed the flirtation and walked off thinking about how bad, and bold she was.

Shortly he met up with Mike, who was coming out of the Carter which was located next door to Bubble's shop.

"What's up, Tim?" Mike greeted him. "New York give you some of that pussy yet?" Mike said referring to Nina.

"Nah Mike," Tim laughed it off. "I ain't fucking with her like that anyway. How was work?"

56

"It was straight, slim. What I owe you for that?"

"That's all you, Mike. You don't owe me shit. I just want you to get some money and stop smoking that shit." Tim said referring to Mike's pcp habit. "Slim, I love you like a brother, you really don't know how that shit makes me feel when I see you out here tripping off that shit."

Hearing Tim speak in the manner made Mike want to straighten up, "I got chu K."

They both looked up when they heard the sound of a roaring engine. Tec came flying up the street on a Suzuki 1300 Higha'Booster.

"What's good slim?" Tec said as he hopped off his bike.

"Ain't shit," Tim said giving him some love.

Mike had a smile from ear to ear, "Tec, let me ride that joint."

"Nigga, you ain't crashing my shit!"

Mike was disappointed, "Tec, you a tight ass nigga." Mike said before he walked off.

Turning his focus back to Tim, "What you doing tonight?

"Im'a check out the Zanzibar. I'm supposed to meet up with this Chinese broad. You should come with me, slim."

Tim didn't respond. He was thinking back to the last time he went out to see a go-go band. Although it was a wild time, it was still one hell of an experience. Just thinking about the way them young girls were shaking their asses while the band played Missy Elliott's 'Get ya freak on' brought a smile to his face.

"Aight slim, I'll meet you there around twelve." Tim said.

Sherrill had just finished her final exams at Duke University, she was excited to be back in D.C. She and her friend Lee were at a bar named 'Jaspers' in College Park, Maryland having a few drinks, enjoying ladies night out. Jaspers was known for having a large friendly happy hour crowd. It was also a hotspot for celebrities. On any given day you might run into a player from the Washington Redskins, or the Washington Wizards.

Lee and Sherrill were really good friends who considered themselves sisters. Ever since her baby's father Moody, got locked up in a big drug conspiracy case, Lee had been dancing at a hole in the wall strip club called the Skylark. After putting money on Moody's books, and taking care of the lawyer fees, all the money he'd left behind was gone just as fast as it came.

Lee knew Sherrill would be upset if she'd found out about her stripping career, but it couldn't be helped. Lee cared about how Sherrill felt, but taking care of herself and her son Lil Moody came first. If she had to, she would sell her pussy to pay the bills. That's the life she was forced to live.

"Gurrrl, do you see that fine ass waiter coming our way?" Lee asked.

"Bitch, you'd have to be blind not to see his fine ass," Sherrill answered. "Shit, I wouldn't mind letting him eat and beat this pussy up, with his fine ass self."

"You too!" Lee smiled then gave her girl a high five.

The waiter walked with a friendly smile on his face. He looked to be in his early thirties, standing at least 6'2, weighing a solid 230 pounds, with shoulder length neat dreads.

"Hello ladies. My name is Tony, and I'll be your waiter for tonight. Can I get you ladies started with some drinks perhaps?" He spoke with good manners, and stood with a firm posture.

Sherrill locked eyes with him, then spoke in her most seductive tone, "Well. Tony I have something you can help with, but it ain't no drinks."

Tony's manhood rose to the occasion, "Is that right?" he matched her stare.

"Yea, that's right. But for now, I'll take a patron silver."

Tony smiled as he jotted down her drink order. Then he turned to face Lee, "And you sweetheart?" he flirted with both women.

"I'll take an apple martini with two olives...and anything else you want me to have." Lee flirted.

My dick down both of y'all's throat, Tony though as he jotted down her order then made his way to the bar.

Sherrill looked him over as he walked away, then turned to Lee and said, "stay in ya lane bitch."

Before Lee could respond, Shawn walked up and wrapped his arm around her. "What's up Lee?"

"Oh... Hey Shawn" Lee said with a smile on her face, and then crossed her fingers. Under the table she hoped and prayed that he didn't mention the Skylark. He was a regular customer, and more so a big tipper.

"How you doing?" Shawn asked as he extended his hand to Sherrill for a handshake.

"I'm fine, and yourself?" Sherrill shot back.

"Shit I'd be a lot better if ole' Lee here stop bullshitting and give me her number."

Lee was becoming upset, "Come on Shawn you ain't never ask me for my number. If you wanted it, all you have to do was ask me for it."

"I was scared, he said with a smile on his face."

"Let me find out, scared money don't make money."

Deciding to change the subject. "So Lee, what you getting into tonight?"

"Me and my girl going to the Zanzibar."

"That's what's up. I might slide through there myself." Looking over at the bar, Shawn spotted his man Rick having a drink. "Well ladies, I have to get going, enjoy your night, I might see y'all later.

Later That Evening

Sherrill stood in her panties and bra looking at herself in a full length mirror. For the past few months she'd been getting up every day at 6:30am and running three miles. From what she could see it was paying off.

She had a flat stomach, perky titties, and hips for days. The only thing that was missing was an ass to go with her hips. I should go to Atlanta and get them shots, she thought while inspecting herself. Her thoughts were interrupted by a knock on the door.

BAM!...BAM!...BAM!... "Sherrill open the door!" Lee yelled.

"Hold on bitch I'm coming. Don't knock my damn door off the hinges.!"

Sherrill opened the door and Lee flew past her like somebody was chasing her with a double barrel shotgun. She went straight to the bathroom.

"Well hello to you!" Sherrill yelled.

"Bitch, I know you heard me knocking," Lee yelled from the toilet seat.

When Lee exited the bathroom, Sherrill was putting on some MAC lip gloss and nodding her head to a KEM cd.

"Bitch is you bout ready?" Lee asked anxious to get her freak on.

Sherrill, complained, "Lee, you know I'm not really with this go-go shit. Niggas be in there tryna grind all on a bitch ass."

"Bitch, please!" Lee laughed at her. "We all know yo ass is a cold-blooded freak."

Sherrill shot back, "Yea that may be true. But a nigga ain't grinding in this ass for free." She turned to face her, "And don't think you slick Ms. Thang. Don't think I didn't notice the look on your face when your boy Shawn came over when we were at Jaspers. All looking like you seen a ghost or some shit. I heard how he be tricking all his money at the Skylark."

Lee dropped her head, "So you…..you know about that huh?"

"Bitch, I been knew. But I wouldn't ever try to stop you from getting your money. You just doing what you have to do. I respect it, you my girl." Sherrill spoke with sincere concern.

"Aww, thank you." Lee said trying to give Sherrill a hug.

She let out a laugh, then pushed Lee away, "Come on now, Bitch. Get up off of me with that mushy shit." She continued to laugh while putting on a Christian Dior tank top and wrap around skirt.

Lee looked her up and down before she spoke. "Girl, you know you wrong as hell. With them big ole titties in that lil ass tank top."

"Bitch, quit hating," Sherrill said rolling her eyes while palming her titts with both hands.

****

Tim pulled up to the club Zanzibar and observed the long line of people outside waiting to get in the club. If he didn't know for a fact that Tec was coming he would have pulled off and went somewhere else. He found a parking spot and whipped his Corvette with perfection on the opposite side of the street, then tucked his 9mm under the seat.

Tim headed over to the VIP line where he saw his ex-girlfriend TT and her sister Angie. He clenched his teeth as he observed both of them dressed like hot bammas. He knew right then that tonight would not go as smooth as he would wish, TT had a bad habit of getting drunk and starting shit in clubs. The last time he'd seen her, she'd poteen tossed out of club Love for acting a fool.

Being the drama queen she was, and knowing it didn't take much to get TT fired up. Angie called out, "Hey Tim! TT wants you."

Being the smooth playa he was, he calmly responded, "Nah, I'm good."

In a drunken slur, TT shouted, "Fuck you then, bitch!"

If it wasn't for TT's fool behavior, she and Tim might still have a chance at being together. She wasn't much of a looker but that pussy was a torch.

As Tim approached the door, he was stopped by the bouncer, "Tim I gotta pat you down," the big black bald headed bouncer spoke.

"Damn, big hulk! What's this all about?" Tim asked feeling disrespected.

"No disrespect Tim, but I got orders to pat everybody down tonight. The owner is watching us like a crazy."

After a quick pat search, the velvet rope was lifted, allowing him to enter the club. Once Tim entered he did a quick scan, seeing if there were any obvious signs of threat. After taking in the scene before him, he made his way to the bar. After placing an order of Cîroc, he turned his attention to finding Tec, and that didn't take long at all. Tec was dancing in the middle of the floor with an Asian chick, she was bad as shit. She wore her hair in a long curly style, the skin tight mini-skirt, had her cleavage bursting out her shirt, off the chinky eyes and lace up Red Bottom heels.

She was killin'em tonight!

She was grinding on Tec like she was a Jamaican Dancehall queen.

He was so into watching Tec that he didn't notice the woman sitting next to him. Off top he could tell that she was tipsy. Looking down seeing her skirt riding up her thick thighs that barely covered her ass. She managed to pull it down a lil bit once she noticed Tim looking at them, but it was too late, Tim already saw the goodies.

He leaned over and whispered in her ear, "I hope you feel as good as you look."

"I hope I look as good as I feel," she licked her lips as she replied.

"I'm Tim,: he extended his hand.

"I'm Sherrill," she responded, then placed her hand in his.

He cleared his throat, "So tell me, what a fine woman likes you doing here sitting at the bar alone like this?"

She shot right back, "I was waiting on a fine man like you to keep me company."

Deciding to cut to the chase, "So how about we exchange numbers so we can hook up? How that sound?"

She licked her lips again, "Yea we can do that."

Tim pulled out his sidekick burnout that he kept handy for moments like this. They exchanged numbers.

"So, Mr. Tim, are you gonna call me tonight?" Sherrill asked.

"Shit, does a bear shit in the woods and wipe his ass with a fluffy white rabbit?"

They both laughed, "You funny, you better call me, if you know what's good for you." Sherrill said then walked away, putting a lil more twist to her hips than usual.

With all that was going on around him, Tim never thought twice about the eyes that watched him from across the club.

"TT, who is that bitch over there talking to Tim?" Angie's nosey ass asked only adding gas to the flame.

"I don't know, but I'm about to find out," TT said as she stormed off in Tim's direction.

Something in his gut told him to look up, and when he did he spotted TT coming his way with a mug twisted up. "Tim, who was that whack ass bitch all up in yo face?" she slurred, making a scene early in the night.

"TT you need to miss me with the bullshit," he said as he tried his best to keep his cool.

"Fuck him TT," Angie yelled knowing she was the cause of all the bullshit.

Tim happened to look back, and the look on TT's face was one he'd seen many times. She was ready to start some shit. All of a sudden, Poe, her baby's father walked up and was pointing in her face. Tim couldn't make out what he was saying, but his mind was already made up that if Poe said anything to him about TT tonight would be his last night on earth.

"Tim, what's up?" Tec asked. He'd noticed the way Poe and the Orlean crew was staring at them.

"Don't even trip," he responded to Tec. With ease Tim pulled out his phone and made a call while keeping his eye on Poe and his crew. Poe was doing too much eye fucking for Tim's taste, and for that he would pay. Dearly!

As soon as the person on the other line answered, "Slim, where you at?"
"Me and Bear riding around. Why, what's up?"

"Look, I need you to meet me out front the Zanzibar. Poe and his crew on some bullshit."

"Say no more, we on our way!"

Tim hung up the phone knowing wherever Mike showed up bodies would drop. He and Tec were walking out of the club when Poe's cousin called Smokey and told him what had happened. He laughed it off as he walked across the street to where Mike and Bear were standing.

"What's up T?" Mike asked as he calmly passed him a Glock 40 cal, totally not caring if anybody saw it or not.

Bear passed Tec a 9mm Beretta, officially arming the entire crew. Mike and Bear both reeked of PCP, but high or not, they were always there for Tim. As people started exiting the club, Tim and his crew were scanning the crowd for Poe, or any of his homies.

"Cuz, there go them bitch ass niggas right there!" Mike yelled pointing to Poe, and his cousin

Smokey. He then whipped out a fifty shot Calico and pulled the trigger.

Baka....Baka......Baka....Baka......Baka!
The shots rang out!

People started to panic and run for cover, not wanting to get hit by the automatic machine gun that was being shot. Mike continued to shoot, having no regard for human life. Innocent, or not, he cared less.

Smokey dove to the ground after being grazed by the chopper that Bear was firing. Poe took off running towards a silver 745 BMW, but Tim was right on his ass, step for step busting shots. A bullet hit Poe in the back, thus knocking him to the ground. Tim stood over him and kicked him in the ass before he spoke, "All this behind a stankin ass bitch slim?" Without even giving him a chance to respond, he squeezed the trigger putting the rest of the clip in Poe's body and face.

He could hear sirens swiftly approaching. As he turned to where the sound was coming from....

"Drop your weapon, now!" A man's voice yelled. "Put your damn hands in the air!"

There was a police officer facing Tim with a gun pointed at his face. With no other choice, Tim dropped the gun, and put his hands in the air. Tim took a deep breath knowing it was all over.

Then he heard.....**Boc....Boc....Boc!**

He looked up and seen the officer falling face first into the concrete. Wasting no time, Tim picked up his gun as he and Tec took off running.

Chapter 5

Tim was riding around looking for Mike when his cellphone rang from his pocket. He pulled it out and saw an unfamiliar number across the screen. "Yeah." he answered with aggression in his tone.

A female's voice spoke in such a soft tone, taking all the anger away from him, "May I speak to Tim?"

"This is him speaking."

"How you doing? This is Sherrill, from the club the other night."

Tim knew instantly who she was, there was too much going on for him to remember to call her. "I'm good shawty, how you doing?"

"I'm good, just got my feet and nails done. About to leave the salon in Hechinger Mall, I was thinking about chu, where you at?"

"I hear that, I was thinking about you too." He smiled from ear to ear as he envisioned her thick legs, and wide hips on top of him.

"If you weren't doing anything, I was thinking maybe we could see each other."

As he was about to speak, he noticed a police cruiser behind him, "Hold on, Sherrill." The police cars flashing lights were on, so Tim pulled over.

The cop drove right past hi. "Hello," Tim said putting the phone back to his ear.

"Yea, I'm right here."

"Aye, why don't you just stay at the mall, I'll be there in about 10 minutes. "

"Alright baby, I'll be in the parking lot in a gold Mercedes. Don't have me waiting."

Tim disconnected the call then drove around the block a few times in search of Mike. But he was nowhere to be found. Finally he gave up, and headed to the mall. When he entered the mall's parking lot, he picked up his phone and dialed Sherrill's number back. Once she answered Tim told her to look for him in a black Corvette. Once he pulled in front of the nail salon he spotted Sherrill sitting on a gold CL500. She noticed him as well, and flashed her hi-beams to get his attention.

He pulled up next to her and rolled down his window, "What's up Sherrill?"

"Just waiting on you." She flashed a sexy smile.

"Can you follow me for a second." He asked eager to see where this meeting would take them.

"Sure, I can do that."

A few minutes later they pulled up on L Street. Tim pulled over and parked in front of the Carter, then blew the horn. Crackhead John was standing there with his eyes big as golf balls, clearly geeking. He had a bucket and some rags in his hands which he sat down when he saw Tim pull up. With a smile on his face as if he'd just hit the Powerball he ran over to Tim's car.

"What's up T?"

"Shit, have you seen Mike?" He asked still in search of Mike.

"I saw him and Bear earlier."

Tim was happy that somebody had seen him, "Ok, cool" Tim looked in his rearview mirror. "John, I need you to go tell the broad behind me that I said to park her car and come get in with me. And also, tell her to give you her keys so you can clean her car," Tim said passing John a twenty-dollar bill.

"Ok I gotchu Tim." John said eagerly putting the money in his pocket. He walked over to Sherrill's car and delivered the message. She was hesitant to give her keys to a fiend, so she picked up the phone and called Tim.

"Tim, is my car gonna be alright?"

"Yea, baby girl trust me. You good." He laughed at the way she showed her nervousness.

Sherrill hung up and passed her keys to John, then she hopped out and made her way to Tim's car. Tim watched her through the mirror, and he had to admit She looked way better than what she did at the club.

"You hungry?" He asked once she got comfortable in the car.

"A lil," she replied looking back at her prized possession. "Tim, you sure my car is gon be aight?"

"Yea, trust me boo."

A few minutes after they pulled off he looked over at her and saw her looking in her vanity mirror putting on some extra MAC lip gloss. He struck up a conversation and they chit-chatted back and forth while riding down the highway. The energy was cool between the two of them. They even sang along to a song that played through the Bose sound system Finally when they reached the restaurant of Tim's choice, Sherrill had a big smile on her face.

"What you smiling for?" He asked.

"Just thinking about how handsome you look, Sherrill flirted with lust in her eyes. She wore a pair of skinny legged hip hugging MS 60 denim jeans, with a red Gucci halter top, along with a pair of open toe sandals showing off her fresh coated French pedicure.

She was looking good and she knew it.

As soon as they entered the restaurant, a waitress approached them.

"Thank you for coming to Moe's. My name is Camille and I'll be your waitress for tonight. Would you like a table or booth?"

"We'll take a booth," Tim answered.

The two were led to the rear of the establishment and seated in a booth by the window. "Can I take your drink orders?" Camille asked.

"Yes, ummm can I have a Tim on the hard," Sherrill requested throwing a sexy look in Tim's direction. "Or if you don't have that, I'll take a Patron Silver."

The waitress smiled before she spoke. "Well, I don't know what the first drink is, but I can definitely get you a Patron. And for you, sir?" She turned her attention to Tim.

"You can bring me a henny and coke."

The waitress handed them a pair of menu's and said, "I'll be back shortly with your drinks, and to take your meal orders."

Once the waitress left, Tim decided to continue the flirting Sherrill had initiated. "Sherrill, you know that if you stay the night with me, I can assure that you'll get that "Tim on hard" that you ordered.

"I guess we'll just have to see about that," Sherrill smirked.

A short while later, the waitress returned with their drinks. "Have you decided what you wanted to order yet?"

Sherrill was sitting studying the menu, but Tim said, "Can I have two stuffed Sherrill breast, and a nice piece of Sherrill fish?"

"Stop it boy! She's talking about something on the dinner menu, nasty." She giggled to the waitress, "Sweetheart don't pay him no mind."
The waitress smiled politely thinking of how wild this couple was, they made her night. Sherrill decided to order a Surf and Turf with a side order of jumbo shrimp.

"How about you sir? Have you decided?"

He wouldn't let up. "I'm still trying to get some of that Sherrill fish, I got a real taste for it, but I'll settle for the same thing she ordered....for now. "

She playfully slapped his arm, "Would you quit it."

The next hour was filled with good fun, and conversation. Mixed with nonstop flirting. Sherrill sat in the passenger seat staring at Tim. She took his right hand into hers and held it, caressing it for the duration of the ride. The night air was cool, and the sound of the V10 engine had her pussy juices flowing. She was really enjoying herself, and not only was Tim nice to look at, he had a cool personality and was fun to be around.

This could turn into something she thought as she listened to the sound of the night.

Vice Squad Detective, Durham walked briskly down the hall of the police station. He stopped at the homicide room 301 and knocked on the door. "Come in," Det. Stone called out from the other side of the door. When he entered the room he found Stone staring at a piece of paper. He was dressed in an all-black suit, a black button up shirt, with his hair slicked back. A gold badge hung from his neck.

"Stone, you good!" Durham greeted his fellow officer, showing concern.

"Awe, you know me," he replied without taking his eyes off the paper. "Just trying to solve another case. What brings you down to homicide?"

He adjusted his stance before he spoke.

"I have something I wanted to run by you, you're the lead on the Gamble case, right?"

"Yes, I am." Stone said as he was trying to figure out what he wanted.

"Well I have a good reason to believe that the Gamble case, may somehow be tied in with the Millers brothers' case. According to one on my many informants overheard someone talking about the Gamble shooting, and apparently Donald and Darrell Miller were the shooters. Word was that, Gamble's brother was putting twenty thousand on the shooter's head of the person responsible for his brother. And I guess he got his man."

Stone sat back and thought about what he'd just heard, his look was unreadable as he took a sip of his piping hot coffee, and this would be a lead worth following.

****

When Tim and Sherrill got back to L street, they saw police cars all over the place, an ambulance and crowds of people flooded the streets. "Sherrill, stay here till I get back," Tim said as he pulled over and hopped out. As he got closer he noticed a pimp by the name of Juju standing on the corner with a few of his hoes next to him. "Ju, what's going on?" Tim asked as he closed the distance between the two.

Juju shook his head before he spoke, "Your man Bear, he tripping off that shit. Smoking that monkey piss got him out'chere tweaking, moe."

Tim looked up the block and spotted Bear, he was asshole naked, balls and dick swinging. The police were yelling at him. Telling him to get down on the ground. Bear was so high, he couldn't understand a word they were saying. The cops stood there confused, trying to figure out the best way possible to take him down with the least amount of force.

They knew when a man was high off PCP.

Finally a few of them were able to take him down and cuff him. Once he was secured in a pair of zip cuffs, he was taken to the station to be processed till he calmed down.

Seeing this, Tim made his way back to where Sherrill was awaiting. Once inside the car, he looked over to her. "I'm sorry for having you around this bullshit, one of my men was tweaking off that boat.

She placed her hand on his before she spoke, "Is he gonna be ok?"

Tim dropped his head, "Yea, he should be. This is nothing new to him," he stared into the sky, looking at nothing in particular. Sherrill knew he was hurt, but she didn't say a word, knowing he'd tell her sooner or later. Tim let out a deep breath, "Let me go get your car keys."

When Sherrill looked over her shoulder, her car was parked right where she'd left it. Her shit was sparkling! It took Tim about ten minutes to find smoker John, then he handed her the keys. "Thank you," she smiled as she took the keys from his hand.

"No problem," he spoke before he cleared his throat. "But check this, I need you to give me a minute to take care of something right quick. Okay?"

"Okay boo."

As Tim walked away from the car he noticed Juju watching Sherrill like a hawk, the look in his eye gave Tim a bad vibe. "Something on your mind, slim?" He asked with a bit of aggression.

"Awe, come on slim. Just being a pimp," Juju replied thinking about how much money he could bring in if he'd had Sherrill on the strip. "Shit you need to let me show you what to do with that." Juju said concerning Sherrill.

"Get your bama ass outta here, I don't need no fake ass pimp with two hoes to show me shit. I'm good slim.

He could tell the comment hurt Juju's feelings. "Yea, whatever nigga. If you see Mike tell him to call me. I'm bout to roll out."

Tim walked away still thinking about his cousin and his whereabouts. He knew Mike and Bear always got high together. So seeing Bear tweaking off that shit, and not seeing Mike raised some concern in his heart. He tried to call Mike's cell once more, only to get the voicemail As soon as he hung up, his phone started ringing in his hand. He answered quickly hoping it was Mike calling back, "Hello."

"What up Moe?" Tec asked.

"Shit, sitting around the way," Tim responded knowing Tec's voice from a mile away. He'd hoped it was Mike. "That nigga Bear was tripping off the wet, had the police around this mah'fucker like shit!"

"Where the fuck that nigga Mike at?"

"Moe, I been calling that nigga phone all fucking day. I 'ma keep trying, but in the meantime I'm on my way to the Days Inn on Annapolis Road with that chick I met at the club the other night."

"You strapped?" Tec asked making sure Tim had his gun at all times.

"Ain't no question!"

"Aight slim, hit me later."

After Tim made a few moves in the Carter he jumped in his car with Sherrill right behind him. Looking in his rearview mirror he was satisfied to see that she was right on his bumper. Making sure he covered his tracks, he pulled out his cell phone and called Niecy. She answered on the first ring.

"Hello."
"Hey boo. You thinking about your man?"

"You know I am baby. I'm missing you like shit."

"Shit, what time you get off tonight?" Tim asked hoping she didn't say right now.

"I was just about to call you when I took my break. I have to work a double shift tonight. Toya bamma ass called out again. I need some dick bad as a motherfucker. "

"Damn, you got a nigga dick hard as shit. I love when you talk like that." Tim played into his act. "I'll come up there right now and hit chu in the car."

Niecy whined, "Baby stop, you making my pussy wet. It's busy up here right now. Let me call you on my break, I'll go to the car and play with this pussy for you."

"Say no more. I love you."

"I love you too, Tim."

Once he hung up with Niecy, he called Sherrill and they flirted back and forth until they pulled into the Days Inn parking lot. They parked side by side, and walked into the lobby hand and hand like a happy couple. Tim paid for a suite, got his keycard and made his way to room 616.

When they opened the door, the first thing they saw was the heart shaped bed. Along with a heart shaped tub with Jacuzzi jets. When Tim turned around to face Sherrill she was stripping out of her clothes and heading to the shower. After seeing her naked, Tim thought about following suit, but quickly changed his mind. Instead, he grabbed the remote and started flipping through channels on the 62 inch flat screen. As hard as he tried to focus on finding something to watch, the sound of the water running, and the vision of Sherrill's naked body all soapy and wet drove him crazy. He looked down and seen his dick was standing at full attention. He took a deep breath and headed towards the shower.

Sherrill peeped her head out the shower when she heard the door make a sound. She smiled when she saw Tim standing there taking off his shirt. "What took you so long?" She licked her lips, "I thought I was gonna have to come out there and get you."

As Tim was stepping out of his pants, his cell phone was vibrating. It was Niecy. He looked at the number across the screen, then stuffed it back in his pants pockets. By now Sherrill had two fingers in her pussy, moaning slightly causing Tim too damn near trip trying to get to her. When he stepped in the shower, Sherrill wasted no time. She grabbed his erect dick and dropped to her knees. Looking up at Tim she took his entire length in her mouth. She continued to lock eyes with Tim as she slurped back and forth. He let out a moan and gripped her hair with his right hand, she didn't resist at all once he started stroking her mouth like it was a pussy. Totally relaxing her muscles in her throat she was able to take all of him.

She did her thang on his dick, then paid his balls some attention. Using no hands she took both his balls in her mouth, then one at a time. She closed her eyes and put his dick back in her mouth and started going in overdrive really working him over. She opened her eyes slightly, then took the dick out and said, "Cum...Cum...In….In my mouth! She continued to slurp and suck, never missing a beat as she kept his dick in her mouth. "I wanna taste you...I want to see how you taste in my mouth.

Tim thought his dick had a mind of its own, as soon as she said mouth he let a load of cum down her throat. He gripped her hair once more and filled her mouth with his seeds. And she drank every last drop, still sucking and trying her best to make him buckle at the knees. She stood to her feet, then whispered in his left hear. "Let's get outta here, I need some of that dick in this pussy. Now!"

She exited the shower before he did, by the time he made it to the room she was on all fours, ass in the air with two fingers in her pussy. "Come fuck me from the back, come get this pussy, daddy." She cooed as she fingered herself. From where Tim stood, he could see how wet and slippery that pussy was. Her fingers were slimy, and Tim was ready to bust that ass!

His dick seemed to grow an extra inch as he watched her please herself to her own rhythm. It was if she was in the room all alone and Tim loved every minute of it. He closed the distance between them and stared at her pretty, bald shaved pussy. He wanted so bad to taste her, but he didn't want to violate the promise he'd made to himself concerning Niecy. Never eat another bitch's pussy, his mouth watered as he thought about it. He slid his dick through her pouty pussy lips and felt the walls of her pussy tighten as he pressed on. He hit her with long and deep strokes, she looked back biting her bottom lip loving every second of the vaginal assault. Once he sped up, she started throwing it back to him, moaning and panting for her breath.

That pushed Tim over the edge.

Think about basketball...Think about basketball, he said to himself as he tried not to skeet too fast. But it was worthless, Sherrill's pussy was just that good. He let off a strong nut inside of her, gripping her waist, pulling her to him with every stroke. She looked back feeling cum oozing through her stomach. She sucked her own titties as she laid across the bed. All Tim could say was, thank you. She looked at him with pure seduction in her eyes and said, "no Tim thank you."

Sherrill woke up the next morning feeling like she was in heaven. After a long night of non-stop love making, she'd labeled Tim the most gentle, most skillful lover she'd had in years. She laid her head on his chest, listening to his heart beat as he slept, she realized at that very moment how comfortable she felt with him.

After soaking in her thoughts, Sherrill decided to get up. She eased slowly out the bed not wanting to wake him. She retrieved her Gucci clutch bag from the nightstand. Then dug around inside until she found what she was in search of, a pre-rolled blunt, and a lighter. She crept to the bathroom like a thief in the night, sat on the toilet and fired up.

When Tim finally came to the strong smell of weed filled his nostrils. I didn't know she smoked, he thought as he didn't remember her saying she did. He could hear her in the bathroom coughing and gagging. Must be some good shit, he shook his head as he sat up in the bed. "Sherrill, you aigh't in there?" He called out, making sure she was okay.

"Yea...I'm okay," she choked between coughs. "You don't mind if I smoke do you?"

He laughed before he responded.

This bitch geekin like shit!

"Nah you good. As long as you ain't smoking no dirt."

"Dirt!" she yelled back. "Nigga all I smoke is Kush!

Sherrill appeared out the bathroom asshole naked with a blunt hanging from her lips. She climbed in the bed and found her spot next to Tim.
"You want some?" She asked making that sexy eye contact once more.

"Depends on what you offering." Tim said with a look of seduction himself.

She took a deep pull then put the blunt in the ashtray, she took Tim's dick in her hand, slapped her tongue with it, and then took him whole in her mouth. For the next twenty minutes she sucked two more nuts out of him, and swallowing every last drop of his cum.

You a muh'fucker Tim said as he slid out the bed, barely making it to the shower.

When Tim ended his shower, he exited the bathroom to find Sherrill sleeping. He then heard his cell phone vibrating from his pants pocket. He picked it up and seen that he had missed nine calls and six of them were from none other than Niecy. He decided to wake Sherrill.

He tapped her on her shoulder, thus breaking her outta her trance. She woke up with a smile on her face. "Hey you," she smiled.

"Boo, I gotta make a run, and handle some shit right quick."

"I understand baby, you think I can see you later?"

"Fuck yea, take your time and when you get up give me a call. I'll take care of the room for a few more hours, okay?"

Quickly Tim got dressed and made his way to the door but not before kissing Sherrill goodbye. She reached out for a hug, and they shared an embrace as if they'd been lovers for years.

As he pulled out of the parking lot his conscious was playing tricks on him. He knew he was wrong for stepping out on Niecy, not to mention she would go bananas if she found out about his doggish ways. He shook it off and pushed those thoughts to the back of his mind, he had to remain focused.

****

Niecy sat in the living room staring at the flat screen, not really caring what was on television. She'd been up all night, not being able to sleep, not knowing where Tim was; or even if he was in jail or somewhere in the city morgue. The worst feeling of any woman is not knowing where your man is at in the wee hours of the night. The only thing open all night are hospitals, jails and another bitch legs!

She heard the engine to Tim's car as he pulled into the driveway. When he opened the front door, he called her name as he entered the house.

She didn't answer!

He could hear the sounds of the television coming from the living room so he figured that's where he'd find her. When he walked in, he found her staring at the television, and he could tell she was pissed. She shot him a look of disgust, then turned her head.

Trying to make small talk to test the waters, he spoke "Hey Niecy, what's up?"

She totally ignored him. She rose to her feet and stormed out of the living room.

The only thing on her mind was knowing that Tim was safe and a warm bed, and some undisturbed sleep. She was simply too tired to argue; she slammed the door behind her and plopped down on the bed.

Moments later, the door flung open and Tim entered to find Niecy in the bed crying. Feeling like shit, knowing he was the cause of the pain she was feeling. He reached out to her. "Bey, what's wrong?" he asked, already knowing the answer to that question.

She let out a grunt before she spoke, "Tim, I'm tired of this shit!"

Instead of trying to mend things and going back and forth, he remained silent. He knew if the shoe was on the other foot and she'd come in the house at this hour, he'd bust her fucking head open.

"Niecy, I'm sorry," he said feeling extremely guilty watching her cry her eyes out. "I know it doesn't make much a difference, but I'm truly sorry baby."

Niecy laid silent, being sucked in by her pain; allowing her tears to flow freely. She didn't know what to make of his apology that was the last thing she'd expected to hear him say. Although she lived and breathed for Tim, she was really starting to become tired of his shit and foul behavior.

She stared him in his eyes then wiped her tears, "Tim, I love you." Her tears seemed to pick up. "You...You...Take my love for granted."

Her words cut Tim deep, and he felt every word she said. He knew this time he'd fucked up!

He thought hard to himself, what the fuck can I do to make this up? I can't be putting these geekin ass bitches before my wifey. You slipping, moe!

Chapter Six

Mike pulled up on M street, anxious to cop some of that shit that had Bear tweaking. He parked his Honda Accord, leaving it running and walked over to a group of guys known for selling PCP.

"Aye, Cricket. Lemme holla at chu slim."

The tall one of the group known as Cricket looked up when he heard his name being called. He recognized Mike instantly. "What's good nigga?" he asked as they shook hands.

"Slim, you still got that man down.

"Yeah , what you need?" he asked as he cautiously looked around for police.

"Let me get one of those."

Mike dug in his pocket and pulled out a wad of bills. He peeled off a twenty and handed it to Cricket. Cricket then reached in his pocket and pulled out a pack of Newport's and an ounce bottle of PCP. He dipped the cigarette in the liquid substance, then handed it to Mike.

"Here you go." Cricket said as he put the product back in his pocket.

"Thanks slim," Mike said as he walked away with the wet cigarette. He briskly walked back to his car, eager to get home to get high. He prepared to drive off, but couldn't.

That monkey piss was calling his name.

He reached in his pocket in search of a lighter. When he couldn't find one he became frustrated. "Fuck!" he shouted as he went from his pocket to the glove compartment. It was there that he found what he was in search of. He put the stick between his lips and set fire. In an instant his mind went back to the conversation he and Tim had a few days ago. He knew he was wrong for getting high again, he shook it off and continued getting high.

Nine pulls later his eyes took on a spaced out look, he sat in the car staring straight ahead in a deep daze. Just when he thought he couldn't get any higher, he took another pull.

Instantly his mind started spinning!

His body soaking wet as sweat started to pour from his head. He started to see shit, images of dead people, and pink elephants, then a dog started barking. He looked over to the passenger seat and the same dog that he heard was sitting in the seat with his seatbelt on; then he has two heads.

Mike jumped out the car, screaming to the top of his lungs. Tripping over his own feet he fell flat on his face. Instead of going to his side, Cricket and his boys sat there laughing and tripping off Mike. Two women in a car passed the scene, seeing Mike on the ground in the middle of the street and instantly thought he'd been hit by a car. They pulled over and called 911. Being that M street was always under some type of watch, it didn't take long for the cops to swarm the block.

Just like roaches when the lights come on, niggas was scattering every which-a-way and Mike was no exception. He might have been tweaking but he wasn't that far gone to not hear a mah'fucker yell five-o. He still knew what time it was. Stumbling to his feet, he rushed a short distance to his vehicle, totally ignoring the shouts of the police ordering him to stop. He jumped in his still running Accord and pulled off. In two point two seconds his rearview mirror was full of red and blue lights.

****

TT sat in her house holding a picture of Poe. She was struggling to hold back the tears and pain. But somehow they found their way down her face. Angie stood over her sister feeling helpless. Although, Angie was known for agitating things, she knew that now wasn't the time for the bullshit. Her sister was mourning and she needed her. Besides, if she said what was really on her mind, and Tim caught a whiff of it. Both of their lives would be in danger.

As the tears finally stopped, TT turned that anger inwards on herself. She'd allowed her affection for Tim to blind her. For years she'd allowed him to get away with things she would never tolerate from another man.

"Angie, Tim killed my baby," she said without thinking.

TT don't say that," Angie cautioned. "You don't know that for sure."

"Angie, you don't know that mah'fucker like I do," TT insisted with venom in her voice.

"But don't worry, he gon get his."

****

Tim had barely been sleep for ten minutes before being disturbed by a ringing cellphone. He looked over and noticed that Niecy was gone. Shaking his head, he reached over and answered his phone.

It was an automated voice service, "This is Verizon with a collect call from Rome, if you do not wish to accept this call please hang up now. To accept this call, press zero now." After pressing zero, the automated voice continued, "Your call is being connected. Thank you for using Verizon."

"Hello," Rome spoke into the phone first.

"What's good?"

"You know me, just taking the good with the bad. Check it out slim, I need you to follow me," he said preparing Tim for the code he was about to speak in. "You know that monkey that was trying to bite you at the zoo the other night? Well, his monkey was running around talking about it."

Tim scratched his head before he spoke. "Is that right?"

"Yeah slim, that's what I been hearing."

Tim decided to change the subject, "so what your lawyer talking about?"

He heard the smile through the phone, "Aye, everything looking good. Thank you for all your support, and everything you've done for me."

"Say no more, I know you would have done the same for me."

"Ain't no question," Rome agreed. "Alright K, I 'ma let you go, I gotta call Trina, I'll hit chu later."

"Aight, Rome. I love you slim."

"Love you too!"

****

Tec was cruising through traffic on his way to the Carter while listening to a Rick Ross cd when he saw a red Land Rover slam on its brakes to avoid running a red light. He pulled up beside the Rover and looked over to see a female that resembled Usher's ex-girlfriend Chili. She looked his way and cracked a smile.

"If he won't I will," Tec said through the open car window trying to sound as smooth as possible.

"Is that right?" she smiled as she responded showing a set of pearly whites.

"Ain't no question. Why don't chu pull over to the Exxon over there so I can holla at chu for a second."

She replied by pulling off when the light turned green, then veered to the gas station. He pulled behind the Rover, reached under the seat and gripped his P89 Ruger and put it on his waistline as he hopped out his sparkling new 750 making his way to the Rover.

When he made it to the Rover, he smiled as he greeted the woman. "How you doing, Chili?" Referring to the R&B singer from TLC.

"I'm fine, but you can call me Ebony."

"My bad, but you look just like her." He continued to smile, feeling every minute of this conversation.

She laughed saying, "I hear that a lot, but trust me, she ain't got shit on me."

"I know that's right." Tec agreed. "So Miss Ebony, when you gon let me take you out?"

She cut her eyes at him, "I don't know for all I know you could be a killah or rapist or something."

He couldn't help but laugh at her comment. "Nah baby, the last thing I am is a rapist, and if I were a killah, I wouldn't kill you. I tell you what, take my number and give me call. How that sound?"

"Sure, I can do that."
After exchanging numbers, Ebony drove off and Tec strolled back to his car. As he was about to pull out the gas station, his phone rang.

It was Tim.

"What's up slim?"
"Tec, where you at?" Tim asked with a bit of urgency in his voice.

Tec sensed something was wrong, "I'm bout to go around the way. "Why what's up?"

"I need you to come over to my joint, slim."

"Aight, I'll be there in thirty."

They disconnected the call. Tec's mind was racing the entire time wondering what was going on. He could tell by his voice that something was wrong. Minutes later Tec parked in front of Tim's house. He hopped out, rang the bell and Niecy opened the door.

"Hey Tec! How've you been doing?" She asked while giving him a hug, then moving to the side to allow him inside.

"I'm good, just taking it easy," Tec responded as he entered the home. "Where my boy at?"

"He's upstairs, hold on let me call him...Tim!" she called out.

Moments later Tim appeared with a disturbing look on his face, "what's good, slim?" Tim asked as he gave Tec a pound. "Tec, you know I hollered at Rome."

Tec's face lit up, "Oh yea. What's up with slim?"

Tim sat down before he spoke. "He said that bamma ass, nothing ass bitch TT been running her mouth about that Poe shit. Joe, I 'ma need you to see that bitch." Tim said with not a tad bit of remorse in his words.

Tec knew this day would come sooner or later, one thing about the streets is that niggas can't keep their mouths shut, so you know a bitch gonna talk. "Consider it done." Tim locked eyes with Tec, knowing he couldn't pay for the type of loyalty he showed.

****

Shawn and Rick were at their favorite spot, The Skylark Lounge, chilling having some drinks and shooting the shit. In the midst of all the women and drinks flowing, Rick turned to Shawn and asked, "Oh yeah, Shawn, you heard about your man Tim?"

"Word on the street is that them people on his ass about that shit at the Zanzibar." Rick gossiped like a bitch in the beauty salon.

Shawn took a sip from his glass, actually happy that this may be the reason Tim may go to jail, or go on the run. "Oh yeah. Fuck that nigga, I was about to stop fucking with him anyway." Shawn said as he put his glass back on the table.

After finishing her set, Lee strutted off the stage. She stopped by a few tables mingling with some of her regular customers before heading over to where Shawn and Rick sat.

Shawn was so caught up in his conversation he was having with Rick that he failed to notice Smokey and two other niggas from the Orleans Crew walk in the lounge and head straight toward the VIP section.

Lee strolled up and kissed Shawn on his cheek, "Hey boo. What's up?"

"What? My money ain't good enough?" Shawn asked flashing a wad of bills.

Lee hopped on his lap, "Come on Shawn, don't act like that."

Her ass was so soft and phat that it was popping out of the dress she was wearing. Shawn's dick was harder than a mah'fucker! After a few songs, Lee left to go mingle some more as she walked off. Shawn was nodding his head to the music when he looked over and saw Smokey and his crew coming his way.

Here we go, Shawn thought as he prepared himself.

"What's up Shawn?" Smokey said while staring him straight in his eyes as if he were looking through him.

"Shit, just chilling." Shawn shot back knowing Smokey was always on bullshit. Rick was about to get up and make his presence known, but quickly decided not to when he saw Smokey's homie Alvin, pat his waist letting him know he was strapped.

Smokey looked back and forth before he spoke, "Nigga, I should bust yo shit!"

Shawn tried to defuse the situation.

"Smokey, what's this all about?"

"Bitch ass nigga, you know what this about!" Smokey yelled. Then he hawked spit in Shawn's face.

It took everything inside of Shawn to stay calm. He picked up a napkin and calmly wiped the spit off his face.

Smokey continued to go on, "Tell ya man Tim, that when I catch his bitch ass, he won't be lucky." Smokey declared before exiting the club.

When Smokey reached the parking lot, he couldn't find it in his heart to let these niggas get away so easily. He and his crew sat parked a few cars over from Shawn's Porsche 911.

Smokey had a frown on his face as he sat holding an AK-47 with two banana clips duct taped to one another. Lil Alvin had an AR-15, while Rex had a MP5 which held eighty rounds.

"You niggas ready?" Smokey asked as he looked around seeing all the guns his squad came prepared with.

Lil Alvin replied by sliding back the hammer, thus making sure he was ready to fire. "You ain't gotta ask me." He replied. Rex just nodded, he wasn't the type for all the talking, and he knew what time it was. He looked up and spotted Shawn and Rick exiting the club. There they go!

The three men hopped out the van like a SWAT team. There was not a word said, they just started shooting.

BAKA...BAKA..BOOM...BOOM..BAKA...B AKA...BAKA...!

The sounds of the automatic gunfire resembled a battlefield in Afghanistan. To the shooters it felt like thirty minutes, in reality in less than thirty seconds Shawn and Rick's bodies lay on the pavement. Lifeless and full of bullet holes.

"Fucking wild'ass nigga thought he was gonna get a pass!" Smokey said before jumping back in the van and burning rubber.

Chapter 7

Vice squad Detective Durham approached room 301 and knocked. A male voice from the other side invited him in.

"Hey Stone! How ya doing bud?" Durham greeted the room's occupant.

"Same ole shit. Working hard trying to solve these murders," Detective Stone replied. "What can I do for you?"

"I have something I wanna run by you."

"Shoot. I'm all ears," Detective Stone said as he wanted to hear what he had to say.

"Well, Stone. I've been investigating a guy by the name of Tim Gamble."

Stone's mind went into overdrive as he thought about the last name. "Wait, is he related to Tony Gamble?"

"Yes, they are brothers," Durham replied before going on. "According to one of my many informants, Tim was the one who put twenty grand on the information to who killed his little brother. And apparently he cashed out when it came back that the Miller brothers were the blame for the shooting."

Stone listened with the rapt attention like a toddler hearing his favorite bedtime story.

"Earlier today," Durham continued, "uniformed officers Jones and Thompson were responding to a call when they noticed a car fleeing from the scene. They gave chase and the car crashed. As they approached the car they took heed to an assault rifle on the passenger side. After taking the driver into custody and running ballistics on the weapon. Get this, turns out it's one of the weapons from the Zanzibar shooting."

"What's the driver's name?" Stone asked.

"A Mr. Michael Washington."

"Washington...Washington...Shit!" He stood to his feet. "I have him made for over a dozen killings, but I can't make the charges stick. No one will testify against this lil shit."

"Why not?" Durham asked eager to know more about this guy.

Detective Stone shot him a glare as if to ask him, 'are you serious'. "Look this guy is feared on the streets of DC every time we build something solid, the witness comes up missing, or they change their story." He shook his head. "That's why!"

"Well, he's still in the hospital."

"Has he made any type of statement?" he paused. "Wait a minute, this guy is ol' school. He's not gonna say a word. He's not like these youngsta's now-a-days, telling on their momma's to get out of jail." Stone made sure his point got across.

"My partner, Det. Tonya Johnson, is posted up outside of his room. As soon as the doctor's give the greenlight, she's gonna question him and formally charge him."

Stone's cellphone started to vibrate from his pocket, he fished around till he located it and flipped it open.

"Hello."

"Hey Stone," his partner Det. Brown said. "I'm at the Skylark. We've got a double homicide down here."

Stone shook his head and let out a deep, "Alright, I'll be there in a second."

From where we stood, he read Stone's body language and instantly knew something big must've happened.

"Bad news!" Durham guessed.

"Yea, double homicide. This city is turning into the wild wild west." Stone stood to his feet and grabbed his walkie-talkie off the desk. "Durham I'm gonna need you to give me a call as soon as Washington wakes up."

"No problem."

Fifteen minutes later, Stone parked a few feet away from the crime scene at the Skylark. The media was all over this, which was always a bad sign for the department. This meant the people are gonna want answers. The crowd was mixed with camera crews and nosy onlookers. Stone noticed his partner talking to a woman who was crying out of control. Not wanting to interrupt, he found a uniformed officer and asked, "What's the story?"

"Two bodies, both with multiple gunshot wounds from high power weapons."

"Any witnesses?"
"Yea, the young lady over there talking to Det. Brown.

When Stone looked over in their direction once more he noticed the panic look on her face, and the way she looked around as if she was nervous for talking to him in front of all these people. He walked over to his partner and whispered something in his ear, then turned to the woman and introduced himself.

"Excuse me miss, I'm Detective Stone," he gently said. "What's your name?"

She eased up automatically knowing she was talking to an officer who had some sense. "My name is Lee...Lee Smith," she responded.

Mrs. Washington was listening to Warren Sapp cd when her doorbell rang. She walked over to the door and checked for whom it was through her peephole. She instantly became uneasy when she laid eyes on two police officers standing there with badges in their hands. She opened the door slightly with the chain still on.

"Good morning ma'am, I'm Detective Phillips, and this is my partner Detective Chambers, we're sorry to bother you but are you Michael Washington's mother?"

Hearing her son's name made her heart skip a beat.

"Yes, why?" she asked trying to figure out what exactly it was they wanted.

"Ma'am, we're sorry to inform you that your son was in a car accident. He's in critical condition...."

"Where is my baby!" She cut him off.

"He's at Washington Hospital Center. If you'd like we can take- his words were cut short by her slamming the door. Quickly she got dressed called her next door neighbor Mrs. Perkins to come watch her 10 year old daughter, Rosetta.

Mike's mom ran into the lobby of the emergency room looking for anyone that could help her locate her son. She rushed to the nurse's station and found an elderly woman sitting behind the counter.

"I'm trying to find my son!" she shouted without a care.

Being used to overly excited people in her days of work, she calmly asked, "What's his name?"

Michael Washington

The elderly nurse punched his name into the computer. As she waited for the screen to come to life she looked at the broken woman standing before her. She was tired of seeing mothers, wives, and grandparents coming to the hospital over the senseless crimes that took over the beautiful place she was once proud to call home. Washington, DC had become a warzone and there was nothing the local police could do about it. The guys on the streets had the same if not bigger guns than they did.

"Are you the mother of Mr. Washington?" Another doctor asked, totally snapping her out of her trance.

"Yes I am," she replied as she dried her tears with the back of her hand.

He extended his hand, then reached in his pocket and offered her some tissues. "I'm Dr. Heinrich, your son was in a serious car accident. He's stable, but unfortunately as it stands right now he may never walk again. However, we're running some test to make sure. As soon as we get the results I'll be able to be more specific on his condition."

Not wanting to hear anymore, the tears continued to fall from her face. "Can you just take me to my baby please?" she asked out of frustration.

Feeling like there was nothing more to say, he agreed and led her to his room. When they entered the room it was silent except for the beeping coming from the machines that were used to watch Mike's vital signs and heart rate. The tears that she'd tried to suppress moments ago found there was down her cheeks once again. The sight of his unconscious body was something she'd never imagined seeing in a million years.

She kissed his forehead then stared up at the doctor. "Please don't let my baby die," she pleaded.

Dr. Heinrich looked at her with sympathy in his eyes, "Ms. Washington, we're doing our best. But ultimately it's up to him. Right now we have him sedated, so he'll be out for a while. It's all in God's hands right now." He cleared his throat, "umm I have a few other patients to check on. Here goes my card, if you have any questions or concerns don't hesitate to call." He put his card in her hand as he exited the room. As he stepped into the hallway he walked past Tim, who was on his way to Mike's room.

When Tim stepped in, the sight of Mike's mother on her knees in prayer broke his heart into pieces. He walked over to her and held her tight, he rubbed her back in support, thus letting her know he was there for her. In all her years of going to church and playing bingo on Wednesday nights, she'd never imagined she'd fall victim to something this hard. She looked up at Tim, and although she wasn't fond of his lifestyle, she was never one to judge. All in all, she was happy to see her nephew. She hugged him tight.

"They saying he won't walk again, Tim." she said as tears started to roll down her cheeks.

Tim's mind went back to the conversation he had with Mike about his smoking habit. The word was already out on the street that he'd been smoking that sherm. He couldn't help but feel slightly responsible for his cousin's condition.

She dried her eyes and looked at Mike for a second, then back to Tim before she spoke. "Tim, even though Mike won't be able to walk, we need to be grateful for the fact that he's still alive."

Tim nodded his head in agreement, but in his mind he was kicking himself in the ass for letting it go this far.

Chapter 8

A Few Days Later...

When Mike finally came to, all he saw was black. It took a minute for his eyes to adjust to his surroundings. When they did the first thing her saw was a female with a short haircut and a body like Kim Kardashian. She was wearing a skin tight business suit, a sleek pair of peep toe pumps. Mike stared her up and down all the way ill he got to the badge that draped her neck.

Ain't this some shit!

"Mr. Washington, I'm Detective Johnson from MPD, she introduced herself. I'm here to charge you with unlawful possession of a firearm. Unless you'd like to help yourself out of this situation."

Mike just stared at her as if she was speaking a foreign language. He was still a lil woozy from the effects of the PCP and medication the doctors been giving him. Yet he still knew exactly where she was trying to go with her subliminal message.

"Look Mr. Washington, she continued, I know all about your reputation as a hardened street thug. You and I both know that you have plenty of enemies that would love to take your spot, or better yet take you out. With you being paralyzed, if and when we lock you up in a federal penitentiary, that would just make the job that much easier."

"What did you say your name was?" Mike asked in a raspy whisper.

She smiled, thinking she was making progress. "My name is Detective Johnson."

Mike looked her dead in the eyes before he spoke, he mustered up all the energy he could as he spoke. "Um Detective Johnson.. I..I need to know one thing." he had a look of sincerity on his face.

She shifted her weight and gripped her pen and paper, "What is it?"

"Do you have on panties?" he laughed then hit the button to get morphine directly to his IV. By the time Detective Johnson was ready to respond, he was nodding out on his way to sleep.

When he finally woke up again, he felt a throbbing in his leg. At first he thought he was dreaming because a paralyzed person shouldn't be able to feel pain in their legs at all. Then he tried to wiggle his toes. When they responded to his brain's command, he knew it wasn't a dream.

An hour later, Detective Johnson walked into Mike's room only to find an empty bed. Needless to say, she was hotter than fish grease. She stepped out the room and looked around in panic. Then rushed to the nurse's station.

"Excuse me, I'm Detective Johnson from MPD ." she said flashing her badge. "Was Mr. Washington from room 112 moved to another room?"

She checked the chart before she spoke.

"No ma'am," she responded.

"Are you sure? Because I just left his room and his bed was empty."

When the nurse indicated that she was sure, Johnson reached in her clutch YSL bag and pulled out her phone to call her partner.

Thirty minutes later they were parked a block and a half away from Mike's mother's house conducting surveillance. They had an all-points bulletin (APB) out on Mike with a quarter of police department looking for him.

Ms. Washington pulled a white STS Cadillac into her driveway and parked. She got out carrying a white plastic grocery bag carrying tonight's dinner when she instantly spotted detectives walking her way. She wrinkled her nose in distaste. Two things she hated in her time of living were cops and rats.

"Ms. Washington, I'm Detective Durham and this is my partner, Detective Johnson," the male spoke.

Cutting to the chase she asked. "Yea..yea what do you want?"

"When was the last time you saw your son?" Durham asked paying close attention to her facial expression. In college he learned in Psychology class how to read lies from the truth in facial expressions and the twitching of the right eye.

Ms. Washington couldn't hold her anger.

"Mah'fucker! The last time I saw him you bitches had him laid up in a hospital bed paralyzed from the waist down!" she snapped with venom dripping from her voice.

Detective Johnson tried to use her card as a woman to bring some calmness to the situation. "Ms. Washington I can feel your pain, but we have a warrant out for his arrest and we need to find him!"

Ms. Washington threw her hands up in surrender. "You can feel my pain?" I know what you can feel. Feel your lips kissing my ass! That's what you can do. Now get the fuck out of my face with that good cop bad cop bullshit." she said like a seasoned vet who's been around this type of stuff before. As she stormed off leaving both of the detectives with dumb looks on their face.

"Fuck that bitch," Durham said. "Let's get out of here and find Washington's black ass. How the fuck did he get out of the fucking hospital unseen?"

******

After escaping from the hospital, Mike immediately hooked up with Tim. They rode in silence as they neared the Greyhound Station. When they arrived Tim parked and killed the ignition.

Tim imagined smacking the shit outta Mike. He wanted to smack him so fucking bad, but even banged up, Tim knew he wasn't going for that shit.

With a look of disgust, "Nigga you letting them mah'fucking drugs control you! He snapped. Mah'fucker you know how I feel when I see you tweaking off that shit? You know how fucked up it felt hearing mah'fuckers tell me how you was in the street screaming and going crazy off that shit? That's some bamma ass shit, slim. We family and we represent each other on these streets." Tim spoke as he reached in his pocket and handed Mike a bus ticket and an envelope with twenty stacks in it. "Take this fuckin money, get ya ass on that bus. When you get to ATL, Jamal's going to get you into a drug treatment program so you can get yourself together. I love you with all my heart slim, but you need help that I can't give you."

Mike reached out and took the envelope with slight hesitation. He exited the car feeling like shit. Although, he knew Tim was speaking the God's honest truth, Mike wasn't feeling the way he was being talked too. So before saying something out of his emotions, he kept his mouth closed and exited the vehicle.

Tim pulled off without a thought of looking back. He loved his cousin, but hated his behavior and how he was weak when it came to drugs. He hoped that some time away and a drug program would help him get his shit together. If only he'd looked in the rearview, he would have seen that Mike never entered the doors of the Greyhound Station.

When Tim finally made it home, the only thing that consumed his mind was a hot shower and some much needed sleep. As he stepped foot in his home the sound of moaning filled the air.

What the fuck, he thought as he pulled his pistol out. I know this bitch ain't crazy he said to himself as he thought about how Ron Isley caught R. Kelly fucking his wife in his own home.

"Ummm...Ummm...shit...Ummm.fuck..." he heard as a lump formed in his throat. He followed the sounds which led him to the living room,. 40 cal in hand, cocked and ready for action he entered the living room with blood in his eyes.

To his surprise he found Niecy on the couch with her legs spread wide open, pleasing herself while looking at the television screen. Tim followed her eyes to see Pinky and Cherokee in a sixty nine position. Niecy had one hand rubbing her clit in a circular motion, while her free hand had two fingers plunging in and out of her asshole.

Tim's dick sprang up in his pants like a jack in the box, He stripped where he stood and joined Niecy on the couch. Face first he ate her pussy, in that same spot they made love for hours until they both fell asleep.

******

On the other side of town Mike was pulling up in a cab on M Street. He hopped out and rushed over to Cricket to buy a twenty dollar stick. As bad as he wanted to stop, the monkey piss was calling his name. Stopping wasn't an option. The drug kept calling him like it had his mental phone number on speed dial.

As soon as Cricket passed him the dipped cigarette, Mike stuck it between his lips and lit it. He took a long pull and held the smoke in his lungs for close to a minute. When he exhaled his eyes were spaced out and he was staring at the sky. He didn't even realize that he was on the ground lying flat on his back.

"Mike!...Mike!..." Jack shouted.

Mike could hear Jack calling him and he wanted to answer but he couldn't. The words just wouldn't come out of his mouth. His vision grew blurry, then the dog in the seat belt appeared again. All of a sudden he started shaking like he was going into convulsions.

*****

Tim was dead to the world when the ringing of his phone woke him. Sitting upright and looking at his Cartier wrist watch, he wondered who the hell could be calling him at two in the morning. When he looked at the caller id and realized that it was hi homie Jack from M street, he instantly knew something was wrong.

"What's up slim?" Tim asked with sleep heavy in his voice.

Jack got straight to the point, "Mike out here tweaking jo."

Tim couldn't believe what he was hearing. "Jack you sure it's Mike?" Tim asked skeptically. "I just put him on a bus to go outta town earlier today."

"Slim, you know I wouldn't waste your time if I wasn't sure."

He took a deep breathe, "Aight, I'll be there in a minute. Keep your eye on him for me please. Don't let him out your sight." he hung up and leaned over to kiss Niecy.

Being on point with her man she instantly knew his mood had changed. "Tim what's wrong?"

"This nigga Mike on M street tripping off that shit again," Tim shook his head in disgust as his words flowed.

Niecy listened and noticed the pain all over his face. After a heated sex session she hate to see him leave. "Tim how long are you gonna be gone?" She asked Jim as she watched him scramble to put his clothes on. One things about women, is they know when their man is about to do some bullshit, and seeing him leave in the wee hours of the morning pained her heart. But he was her man and she played her position.

"Not long. I'll call you when I'm on my way back home. I promise."

Niecy wrapped Tim up for a hug. She didn't want to release her grip. "Be safe."

Tim was furious as he sped through traffic like a lunatic. When he got to M street, he hopped out the car and walked to where Jack was standing. His temper went from simmer to boiling hot after seeing Mile stretched out on the ground, stuck off the PCP. Tim shook his head and his anger was obvious as his eyes were bloodshot red.

Tim loved Mike like a brother, but before he let the drugs kill him, he'd kill him himself. Tim closed his eyes and massaged his temples as he contemplated his next move. Reaching for his waist, he grabbed his glock .45 and aimed at Mike's head.

Pop!...Pop!...Pop!...Pop!...Pop!

He dumped five slugs into Mike's face and chest with no hesitation as if he were a stranger in the street. Jack stood there frozen, He couldn't believe Tim has just done that as if Mike meant nothing.

Tim looked at Jack, before he walked away. "You ain't see shit right?"

Jack, shook his head. "I ain't see a mah'fucking thang, slim." Jack watched the tears roll down Tim's face as headed back to his car.

The Next Morning

Tim's mom called and asked him to meet her over Mike's mother's house. When he pulled up there were cars parked and double parked all the way up the street. He hopped out of his car feeling the beginning of remorse. As he entered the home, the first thing he noticed was family members he haven't seen in years all sitting around with tears running down their faces.

Seeing the amount of stress Mike's death caused to the family really put Tim in a fucked up head space. If only Mike had gotten his ass on that bus, he'd still be alive. Tim thought as he looked on feeling like shit for his actions. If only I could turn back the hands of time, I wouldn't have pulled the trigger. His inner voice said as tears started forming in his eyes.

Chapter Nine

Trina pulled into a huge parking lot in the downtown DC area and parked her BMW. She checked her MAC lip gloss in her vanity mirror then gave herself a once over before she stepped out. Satisfied with how the DKNY pant set hugged her curves, she strutted her way inside.

Her Sergio Rossi six inch heels clicked against the marble floor as she approached the front counter., "Can you direct me to Mr. Tutts office, please?" she asked the receptionist at the desk.

She looked up from her computer screen, taken back by how beautiful Trina was. "Umm if you go down the hall, it's the last door on your left." she replied.

When Trina reached the door, she saw Harry Tutt's name in large letters on the door. She entered the office and saw a middle aged secretary who resembled Vanessa Williams sitting at the desk. "Can I help yo?" the Vanessa Williams look alike asked in a warm tone.

"I'm here to see Mr. Tutt."

She gave Trina a once over as she spoke, "Is he expecting you?"

Just like two cats in a cage, the eye contact was obvious. The thing about two women in the same room, whether one is better looking than the other, or they both may be of the same caliber. One of them has to have something over the other. Trina peeped her scooping her heels out, but didn't feed into her bullshit. She was here for one thing and one thing only. Getting Rome out of jail!

She stood firm as she replied, "yes he is."

She sucked her teeth as she reluctantly sent Trina to the back of the office where she found Harry sitting at his desk.

"Trina! How are you?" Harry asked warmly greeting her.

"I'm doing fine." Trina replied.

"That's good to here, come on have a seat."

Trina sat across from Harry and took a deep breath, She reached in her purse and pulled out a check for three hundred thousand dollars. She could care less, even if it meant draining her entire life savings to get Rome out of jail. She was game for whatever needed to be done, except for one rule instilled her before he went to jail and served a life sentence for an armor truck robbery which led to five officers losing their lives.

It was like yesterday to her memory, her father was known for his play a lifestyle and no matter what he always spoiled her rotten. He would kneel down eye level and tell her life's lessons. But this particular day he told her: "Daddy has to go away. When you decide to give yourself to a man make sure he's a man's man, and will take good care of you. Stand for what's right and always take his own weight for his actions." So since then, snitching has never been an option to her.

Mr. Tutt snapped her out of her daydream.

"Is everything okay?" he asked.

She shook her head, I'm sorry. Umm, should this cover everything?"

"Yes this should do it." Harry said as he looked at the check. Harry neither liked nor disliked Rome. Their relationship was based on the power of the almighty dollar. Nothing more nothing less. Rome, knew exactly where he stood with his lawyer. If it came down to him going to trial against the United Stated of fucking America, he was determined to have the best on his side.

Mike's Funeral

Tim, his family, and his friends filled the funeral home. It was a sea of tear stained and anguish filled faces. All of Mike's close friends were there except for Bear. Mike and Bear were like peanut butter and jelly; you rarely saw one without the other. They'd been that way since meeting at the

Oak Hill Juvenile Detention Center when they were both only twelve years old. After scanning the crowd for the umpteenth time and still not seeing Bear, Tim was nearly consumed with rage.

Later that night

Bear's mom and teenage sister were sitting in the living room of their home watching the latest series of Love and Hip Hop. As they both let out a laugh from something they both found funny on television, they heard a loud boom. The front door of the house flew off the hinges, and Tec and Tim rani n with their guns drawn. Both women screamed to the top of their lungs.

"Shut the fuck up fo' I kill y'all asses!" Tec barked as we waived his gun at both their heads.

Tim looked at the mother and pressed his gun against her forehead, "Where the fuck is Bear?" he shouted, "don't fucking lie!"

"I...I...I don't know." she stuttered in fear for her life. "I haven't seen him.. I. In over....a...week. I swear to God!"

The daughter cried out again after seeing the terror so clearly written on her mother's face. Tec put the gun to the back of the girls head, gripped her by her shoulder length hair. He smacked her in the back of the head with the butt of the gun.

"Ahhhgggg!" she screamed in pain. He gripped her by the neck and jammed the gun in her mouth, almost causing her to throw up. He looked over to her mother.

"Bitch if you don't tell us where Bear is, you gonna have to bury both of your kids!" he threatened.

After seeing the back of her daughter's head leaking from the blow of that gun, mixed with the way these two men came in her home. She knew they were dead serious. There was only one decision to make. "Okay, I know where my son is. But you have to promise to let me and my daughter live after I tell you." Tec shook his head as she began to tell them where her son was hiding at.

In less than five minutes, they had the exact location of where Bear been hiding at. Satisfied with the information and how well it flowed out of her mouth. Tec put his gun back on his waist. The mother let out a sigh of relief at the sight of Tec putting his gun away. Then instantly he snatched her daughter's neck side to side, then snapping her neck like a rag doll.

"Oh my God!" she yelled seeing her lifeless daughter falling slumpt over the couch.

"You said you was gonna-..."

Boc!..Boc!

Tim fired two shots into the back of her head.

Bear had been hiding out at his brother's house way out in the sticks. He felt a certain amount of safety by being so far away from the city. He hoped that Smokey would kill Tim and Tec, or hopefully Detective Durham would use the information he gave him to put them away for life. Til then he was a sitting duck just waiting for something to happen.

Feeling restless, Bear decided to walk to a nearby store to purchase a pack of Newport's. Returning from his walk, he was sticking his key in the door when he heard something that made his blood turn to ice in his veins.

"Well look at the fleas on ol'fluffy," a man's voice said.

Bear damn near shitted on himself as he recognized Tim's voice. He turned toward the voice looking like a deer caught in headlights.

Boc!...Boc!...Boc!...Boc!...Boc!...

The sound of Tim's Ruger filled the air as Bear's body fell to the ground. Looking to his right, the sound of someone opening the door caught his attention. It was Bear's brother coming to see what was going on. "Bear, you busting that damn gun again… I told you-.." was the last words he got out as he opened the door and met the flash of a cannon.

Boc!

One single shot through his right eye took him out of his misery.

Tim recognized weakness in Bear a long time ago, and would have been killed him if it wasn't for Mike. Tim always suspected that if the feds caught Bear at the right time he would spill his guts. When Bear didn't show up at the funeral, instantly his antennas went up. He immediately contacted a female associate of his who worked at the Fifth District Police station. She informed him that the day Bear got arrested, he sang like a bird. Bitch ass nigga told everything he knew, and just like a lot of these rat ass niggas in the street, he thought he was gonna get away. But, from that day forward he was living on borrowed time, and his clock had just run out.

*****

Niecy was driving over to the Cheesecake Factory on Connecticut Avenue to grab her favorite cheesecake and slushy. After that she planned on heading over to Georgetown to cop a dress and pair of Giuseppe Zanetti heels she'd seen last week.

Smokey and his man, Alvin, were a few cars behind her. They'd been trailing her since Smokey spotted her truck stopped at a light on New York Avenue.

Niecy pulled up to the Cheesecake Factory and found a parking spot in the back of the lot. She hopped out the BMW X5 wearing a pair of skinny legged Alexander Wang jeans that hugged her curves to the letter. The clingy BCBG Max top she wore showed just enough cleavage to stop traffic. Not to mention the Vivienne Westwood sandals that showed her flawless french tip pedicure. And this was an off day for her, but still she was looking like a runway model.

Alvin stopped the stolen van a few cars away from where Niecy was parked. The windows were heavily tinted, so they weren't worried about being seen. Pulling the hoodie over his head, Smokey stepped out and began power walking to catch up with his mark.

Niecy being a hustler's wife and living the lifestyle she lived; Tim always told her to be aware of her surroundings. She heard footsteps then turned to see what was going on behind her. As soon as she turned around, she was hit hard with a blow to the mouth, causing her to stumble. Smokey wasted no time hitting her once more with all he had, thus knocking her to the ground.

Niecy was woozy from the sudden attack, but that didn't stop her from fighting back. She went into attack mode, she started punching, kicking, and scratching like a cat in heat. She went harder than she ever went in her life. Although, she was still dizzy from Smokey's punches, people often mistook her looks for being soft. Her favorite line as don't let the cute face, tight waist, and pretty face fool you. Her arrest record was long enough to fill up the Yellow Pages. Growing up in the slums, and one of the roughest projects in DC 'Barry Farms' she never forgot where she came from.

Smokey, on the other hand didn't expect Niecy to put up this much of a fight. He was about to reach for his weapon. His first thought was to kick her ass, but now that the tables had turned, he wanted to kill the bitch.

The sound of sirens from afar brought him back to reality.

It's time to go! He thought as he broke loose and took off running toward the van. Niecy managed to get a good look at the van as they sped off.

As she turned around DC's finest was pulling up to the scene. They tried to get a statement from her, but it was a waste of time. The only person she wanted to speak to was Tim. On her way home, she debated exactly what she wanted to tell Tim. She knew he had zero understanding. Plus he had so much going on she was hesitant to add to his worries. Niecy knew what Tim was capable of and didn't want to be the reason he took a life, or got himself killed in the process. Nevertheless, she knew she had no choice in the matter but to tell him.

*****

When Niecy pulled into the driveway, her hands began to sweat profusely. When she opened the door to her home, for some reason Tim was standing right there in her path and instantly took notice to her face.

"What happened to you?" he asked with his face turned up. He noticed the bumps and lumps on her face. As bad as she wanted to brush it off, she knew he wasn't gonna go for it. The tear that ran down her face caused the makeup to smear, as Tim continued to question her.

"Niecy who the fuck did this to you?!" Tim demanded.

"Baby don't worry about it," she said trying her hardest to prevent the only man she loved from hurting someone because of her.

Tim became irate, "Niecy, I'm gonna ask you one mo'fucking time!... Who did this to you!" Her mind instantly went to the night she woke up and specs of blood were on the carpet and on Tim's shoes and clothing. The same night that the men responsible for killing his brother were found shot to death.....

I have to tell my man what happened, she thought as she lowered her head and the words began to flow.

Later that Night

"What you wanna do?" Tec asked as he and Tim sat up in the living room loading up clips to their weapons. "If we move on Smokey right now, he'll be expecting it."

Tim always being the thinker of the crew. Even as a child he always had the great ideas and somehow always came out on top. He always had the ability to conceal his true intentions. Growing up his mother instilled the game of chess into his mental rolodex. She taught him to think long and hard before making a move, but always think two steps ahead. She would always say "The game is chess not checkers, once a bad move is made, it can't be taken back. That one move could set the game on an irreversible path." He sat and contemplated those lessons, he thought about what had taken place with Mike.

"Yea, you right." he agreed. "We'll wait for now, But when the time is right. I'm gonna touch everything he loves. I'm gonna destroy everything he touched!"

He meant every word he said. Niecy was off limits, and now he was gonna show niggas on these DC street just what that means.

Chapter 10

Smokey paced back and forth in his one room apartment in Riverdale, Maryland. He knew he'd fucked up, and was to the point of no return. He glanced at the picture of his parents that hung over his bed and shook his head. If his intuition served him right, their lives were in danger. He failed his kidnap attempt on Niecy, and knowing that he was fucking with a killer; his loved ones weren't safe.

"Fuck!" he yelled.

Smokey needed to get high. Although he had a twenty dollar bag of 'Hydro' he didn't have any blunts. He grabbed his car keys, then jumped in his Navigator. As he drove to the nearby 7/11 he couldn't help but hear his inner voice telling him he'd fucked up. After running inside to grab some blunts, chips and a two liter of Sprite he made his way back home. Smokey was so preoccupied in his thoughts that he didn't take notice to the tinted out Camaro sitting a few yards from his home.

Pulling into his assigned parking spot, he killed the engine. Letting his thoughts continue to roam before he knew it he was twisting one of the blunts. As he perfected and twirled the blunt through his lips, he was ready to smoke. It was something about 'hot boxing' in a car that made getting high better. He reached in his glove compartment to get a lighter when all of a sudden his driver and passenger door flew open at the same damn time. His first thought was to reach for his 357 Revolver under the driver seat, but the feeling of cold steel pressed against his head changed his mind.

"Don't move bitch!" the shorter of the two gunmen spoke.

Smokey knew he'd been caught slipping, with that being said he did as he was told. The shorter man kept his gun trained on Smokey's head while the other one ruffled through the SUV. He not only found the gun under the seat, but he took the blunt Smokey was rolling.

Ain't that bout a bitch!

Smokey was then pulled by his shirt to the Camaro. "Nigga get you bitch ass in the trunk!" He shoved Smokey to the open latch. "I'll blow ya fucking brains out, slim!" the gunman known as Rosedale Rell instructed him.

Before driving off and making sure Smokey was secured in the trunk, Rell pulled out his cellphone and made a call to someone who was very happy to hear from him. He said a few words as a smile creased his face. He then looked at his partner in crime and nodded his head. He then popped the trunk, and the look on Smokey's face was of pure panic.

"Watch out," his partner in crime said as he lifted a cement block and brought it down on Smokey's head, knocking him out cold. "That should do it." They both burst out in laughter....

Smokey woke up a short while later only to find himself hogtied in what looked like an abandoned basement. His head was spinning and still in pain from the cement block he'd had thrown on his head, from what seemed like hours ago.

"Aye he woke up finally." Rell said as he approached him and smacked him across the jaw with his weapon. If it was up to Rell, he would have been sent Smokey to his maker, but he had to restrain himself because he was acting on someone else's behalf.

The sound of a door being opened made everyone in the room look in that direction, and when Smokey realized who it was , he knew it was over for him. The look in Tim's eyes was one of rage and terror.

"Mmm, mmm, mmmph....," Smokey tried to plead for his life through his gagged lips.

"Untie his feet, Tim swung a short right hook to his face that sent him stumbling backward with blood pouring from his broken nose. Tim delivered another punch, this time to the stomach. The sound of the impact was one that let you know a few ribs have been broken. Going into the rage of a madman, he swung again, and again, and again. His intentions was to make Smokey feel it, and kill him with his bare hands.

Out of breath, Tim spoke. "So what...you..you was gonna rape her?" he asked with a deranged look on his face. Smokey's face was mangled and beyond twisted. He was fucked up!

His head lumped up and both eyes were swollen shut, but Tim wasn't done yet. Rell looked on as if he was amazed by what was taken place before his eyes. Tim began looking around like a crazed animal, his eyes lit up when he seen a broom lying in the corner of the basement.

Going over to grab it, he stood eye to eye with Smokey. "Strip this nigga!" Tim shouted. Rell being the loyal goon, he did as he was asked. Moments later a bloody Smokey stood butt ass naked as if it were his first day on earth, minus the bumps and bruises. Tim stood within earshot of Smokey and asked him again, "So you and your niggas was gon' rape my bitch?...You know I hate rapist, and I got something for your bitch ass nigga." Tim was gone off revenge. The mere thought of someone touching a hair on Niecy's head was enough to drive him crazy.

He walked circles around Smokey until he was dead behind him. Broom in hand he wasted no time jamming it as hard as he could between his ass cheeks. Smokey's eyes lit up, and he tried his hardest to scream behind his restraints. Tim continued to push the broom deeper and deeper each time. He even went as far as banging the broom handle with the butt of his gun. Tears ran down Smokey's eyes, and finally he defecated on himself. Shit poured from his ass like a faucet.

The smell of death was in the air, and Tim felt no remorse. For he knew if they'd successfully snatched Niecy, she would have been beaten and tortured the same way. After Tim was satisfied with bringing Smokey to his knees in pain. He aimed his .45 ACP at Smokey's left eye. "An eye for an eye." **Boom!** He fired a single shot through his eyeball. Then aimed at the other eye and did that same. **Boom!** "Tooth for a tooth!" he shouted then stuck his gun in the deceased Smokey's mouth and emptied the entire clip.

Tim looked at Rell, and his partner, Papa. "Make sure he's never found." Tim said out of breath, as he exited the basement. Rell and Papa just looked on as they went into cleanup mode. Papa new a park in southeast DC where there were wild dogs, and that's where Smokey was on his way too. The dogs would have a good time eating the remains of a human body. Rell rolled out the laced carpet and they went to work, like they were paid to do.

From that moment on, Rell and Papa had a newfound respect for Tim. Seeing a nigga out in work, is much different from hearing about it. And from what they just seen, they knew Tim was not to be pissed off.

Chapter 11

Rome couldn't believe that he was finally home. As soon as they entered the house Trina took off running towards the bedroom. Before following behind her, he kicked off his Prada sneakers that she'd brought him to come home in, and stripped ass naked. He stood there for a minute, allowing his thoughts to set in. His feet sunk into the deep cushion of the Persian Rug he'd purchased not long ago. He looked around and did a quick inventory of his home and all the nice things he had to live for.

I never wanna leave this place again, he thought as the memories of jumpsuits, prepaid phone calls, and half cooked meals stained his memory. It dawned on him that he'd be willing to give up all these material things, to have his freedom. He told himself that he was done with the flashy lifestyle. The presidential Rolexes, the platinum earrings, bracelets, chains, and pendants. He also made a promise to sell all his cars as soon as they were all released back to him. After seeing two men kiss each other like they were a couple, it made him realize just how much Trina meant to him. With that being said, he entered the bedroom.

When he opened the door, Trina was laying naked on their king sized bed. He stood there for a second admiring her flawless body. When he went to join her, he began sucking on her nipples, then slid his tongue down to her naval. He put his hands under her, thus gripping her ass cheeks, and raised her clit to his mouth.

Rome, took his time and ate Trina's pussy like Mr. Marcus in his prime. He wanted to make sure she as nice and ready before he entered her. After her third nut, she was dripping wet and Rome was ready to deliver. He entered his entire dick into Trina's love nest, not stopping until he touched the back of her walls.

He started off slow stroking Trina, but it felt so good, wet, warm and tight that he sped up against his will. Trina was in tune, throwing it back and meeting him stroke for stroke. The sound of their loving sounded like a round of applause. They moved so well together as if they were partners in 'Dancing With the Stars' and would receive all tens for their performance.

The sounds of her moans drove Rome crazy as it always did, but today was different.
"Ohh...oh...sh...shit...give... it...to...me....daddy," she began to shiver and shake.
"Cu...cu....cum...I...in...me...ba...by!" she screamed as Rome felt himself about to explode, and that's exactly what he did. He bust his most backed up nut all in Trina's insides. His knees buckled and he continued to stroke, never missing a beat, and managed to keep his dick hard for three more

rounds. That's something he learned from reading the latest issue of 'Curve' magazine.

* * * * *

Later That Evening....

Tim sat in a warehouse in Silver Spring, Maryland full of handpicked hired goons, There was of course Rosedale Rell, and his partner Papa, Steve Perry from Southeast and 21st Street Pie. They were all vicious, cold blooded killers who enjoyed what they called an easy day's work. They were joined shortly by Tec, who entered the room carrying a crate full of assorted weapons. The crate held everything from AR 15's to MP5's to Glock .45's, 357's and Carbon 15's.

Tim stood to his feet before he spoke, clearing his throat he spoke loud and clear, "Listen up niggas! Y'all already know what we here fo. We bout to take it to them Orlean niggas! I want every last one of them niggas dead! I don't care if they walking with their kids to school, or they mama to church on Sunday! I want them dead. If they helping an old lady across the street, I want them all dead!"

After Tim finished giving his orders, the men began choosing their weapons from the crate. Rosedale

Rell was the first to grab his gun of choice. He picked up a SKS fully automatic with two banana clips duct tape to one another, each holding seventy shots. The grin of death was on his face as he placed the gun into a lawn chair bag. Tim sat back like a proud dad as he watched the smallest nigga in the room, grab the biggest gun in the arsenal.

Papa refused to be left out. He reached and grabbed a Mac-90. He stared lustfully at the gun as if it were a butt naked stripper. It was something about an automatic gun that drove Papa to want to bust more shots. He looked over to Rell, and both of them smiled at one another.

"On my mama, moe. Kill them nigga's gon die tonight, Moe!" Rell said knowing Papa was ready to put some work in.

21st Street Pie chose the Carbon 15, while Steve gripped the AR15. Steve was the type of nigga who didn't care if there was only knives in the crate, he was just ready to fuck something up. Coming from an infamous bloodline of killers, and doing time in Lorton, Big Sandy and Pollock United States Penitentiary's. His gun and knife game was turned up. His name was well known throughout the city for putting in work, not to mention he as the nephew of DC'S most notorious killer.

Tim waited till everyone was done choosing their gun of choice before he reached under his coat and pulled out a sawed off double barrel twelve gauge. Tec came to the party with a date, well two. He had two twin Smith & Wesson .45's.

"Tec , I need you, Steve and Obie down at the end of the block. When shit jump, y'all fuck everything up moving down there. We gonna come from the other end, basically setting up a trap barricade. They run to you, they dead, they run to us, they dead. Either way they all gonna die. No slip ups, and everybody focused. No drugs! Y'all can smoke that shit later!"

Tim requested coinciding with Tec's intentions from their previous plan which was to kill, kill, kill. Tec hated the New Orleans niggas just as much, if not more than Tim. So this was something that he'd been waiting to do for a long time.

Once everyone was armed, and had the plan laid out. They hopped in the two tinted out SUV's and sped off to get it popping. The SUV's were silent as everyone had murder on their minds. It was too late to turn back now, and everyone in them vehicles were not to be out done. Tec hopped out with a .45 in each hand, shooting, them at the same damn time. One minute Fat Chucky was sipping on some liquor thinking about his man Smokey, the next minute he was running scared for his life trying to escape the barrage of bullets coming his way. Then he made the mistake of reaching for his gun. Fortunately for him Tec's bullets hit him in the head killing him instantly. He never felt a thing. On this day chaos reigned supreme on the block. The Orlean crew got caught totally unaware, and most of them got dropped before having a chance to even think about fighting back. Rex and lil Alvin were the only two that mounted any type of resistance, As soon as the shooting started Rex dove behind a parked car, When he came up he was blasting a Tec 9 with an extended 32 round clip.

Lil Alvin took cover behind a mailbox before producing a Desert Eagle with an infrared beam. He started sending hollow point 44 slugs at Tim's group of hired killers. Papa had been consumed by bloodlust making him careless. He was so intent on spraying the car that Rex was hiding behind, that he never noticed lil Alvin drawing his gun on him. The bullets from the desert eagle hit Papa in the back and exited through his chest leaving behind a hole big enough to plant a tree in. When Rell saw his partner drop he snapped. Ignoring the bullets flying around him, Rell walked steadily towards the area Rex and lil Alvin were hunkered down in. He held his finger down on the trigger of the SKS while sweeping it from left to right. Unlike those from Papa Mac 11, the bullets from Rell's SKS tore through the car and mailbox as if they were made of nothing more than paper. By the time he reached them, Rex was dead, and lil Alvin was fast on his way to join him. For good measure Rell stood over lil Alvin and emptied the rest of his clip into his face. Once he was satisfied that both of them were dead, he ran over to check on his man. Papa had managed to turn himself over onto his back, but it was obvious from the frothy blood escaping his mouth that he didn't have much time left.

"Hang on Moe!" Rell pleaded. "I 'ma get you some help."

But it was already too late. Papa squeezed Rell's hand one time and then a death rattle parted his lips. Rell's one rage all over again, but there was no one to take it out on. The Orlean crew had been eradicated, not a single one of them was left breathing. Tim side wasn't without its own casualties. Along with Papa, Steve Perry had been killed. He'd been overly confident and had ended up running directly into Rex line of fire. Tec had been grazed with a bullet, but it wasn't serious. The survivors jumped into the SUV's and sped away knowing it wouldn't be long before the police showed up. Tim was experiencing the worry of a parent worrying about on the their children. He flipped open his cell phone and called Tec in the other SUV, concerned about the way he was leaving as he got into the vehicle.

"You alright slim?" Tim inquired.

"Yea I'm good, I got hit and it knocked the wind out of me, thank God I have my vest on. But Papa didn't make it." he added.

"Damn! Put Rell on the phone."

"Hold on for a second." Tec said she passed the phone to Rell.

"Yeah?"

"Rell, I'm sorry about your man. He was a good dude. I 'ma have Tec give you your man fifty thousand along with the fifty I was gonna give Papa, and whatever Papa family need for the funeral I got that too.

"Okay slim," Rell responded hollowly. He was still fucked up in the head about losing his best friend.

"Put Tec on the phone."

"Yea?" Tec said

"Make sure you get rid of that cell and all them guns. I hit you later!"

"Cool"

Rome sat up in bed staring at Trina magnificent figure, as she walked toward him. She was butt naked carrying a breakfast tray loaded with all his favorites: turkey bacon, beef sausage, french toast, waffles, cheesy eggs, orange juice, and a bowl of fruity pebbles with milk. Trina's plan was to cater to Rome, giving him anything his heart desired.

"Is that for me sexy?" Rome said already knowing the answer

"Yes baby" Trina replied setting the tray on the bed next to him.

"Thank you boo." Rome said appreciatively. He was hungrier than a Muslim at a pork farm.

"Anything for you babe." Trina said in a seductive tone.

"Anything?"

"Anything big daddy, matter of fact when you finish your breakfast, I have some dessert for you."

"What kind of dessert you have for me miss thang?"

"Some sweet booty pie." Trina said as she slid her finger between her thighs and into her moist pussy. "You want some now?"

Rome nodded his head up and down as he stuffed a piece of bacon in his mouth. He ran his eyes up and down Trina's body as he moved the food tray to the nightstand. He was fiening for her pussy like a crackhead geeking for rocks.

Trina laid on the bed next to Rome stretched out on her back, as he kissed her on the lips. Then he moved down and begin tenderly sucking on her hardened nipples. He stuck his fingers inside of her pussy as he let his tongue travel down to her belly button. Finally, he lifted Trina legs and entered her parted pussy lips.

"Hell"

"Yea you like this dick, don't you?" Rome said ramming his dick like a jackhammer in and out of Trina juicy pussy.

"Hell yea!" Trina moaned in pleasure. She loved Rome dick like a rich man loves money.

Rome pulled out of Trina and spun her around so he could enter her from the back. Trina threw it back at Rome as he rode her like a thoroughbred in a Kentucky Derby. He could tell by the way she was shaking and screaming that she was having an orgasm. Rome tried to hold out as he felt himself about to explode, but it was no use. He cried out in ecstasy as he skeeted enough cum in her to flood the White House. Embarrassed that he didn't last longer, Rome collapsed on the bed, exhausted and spent. Although Trina wasn't ready to stop having sex, she was happy to get what she got. And now that it was over, she was grateful for the chance to cuddle up with her man. The next day Rome was channel surfing when he saw something that stopped him cold. It was a news broadcast, on the killing of the Orlean crew. Rome only caught the tail end of the broadcast so he hurriedly flipped to another news channel. But he had no need to worry, news of the killings was on every channel and plastered all through the Washington Post.

"What the fuck!" Rome shouted in shock.

He knew Tim and the Orlean crew were beefing, and by the way the news described the scene, he had no doubt as to who was behind the massacre. Even if Jesus Christ himself would've said that Tim wasn't involved, Rome wouldn't have believed him. Rome grabbed his cell phone off the nightstand and dialed Tim's number. The phone just rang without an answer. It was very unlikely Tim not to answer his phone. Unless of course his battery was dead. That was the only reason Rome could come up with that didn't involve assuming the worst.

Homicide Detective Stone sat at his desk with his arms folded. He was contemplating the reason behind the sudden wave of murders plaguing the area. Even without a snitch, it didn't take a rocket scientist to figure out who was responsible for the deadly massacre on Orleans street. He'd already assembled a team of special officers to apprehend those who were responsible. With an arrest warrant issued for Tim, Detective Stone had every available officer searching for him from sun up to sun down. There were officers searching and roaming L street from the top to the bottom. The Carter, however was quieter than a library.

Ever since the failed kidnapping on Niecy, Tim made sure that every time she left the house, he was with her. Presently, they were seated at a table in the Houston Restaurant located in Rockville, Maryland. This was Niecy favorite restaurant. She loved the way they marinated their Hawaiian steak making it as tender as a newborn baby ass. Tim was staring at Niecy thinking of how he would have never forgiven himself if she would have gotten hurt behind him. When his phone rang he was hesitant to answer it because he was trying to enjoy some quality time with wifey. But, when he heard Baby's Number One Stunner ringtone he knew he should probably answer. It was Dat calling and he probably had the $150,000 dollars he owed and more.

"Ti...Ti...Ti...TIM! Where you aaat?"

Tim bust out laughing thinking about how it damn near took Dat five minutes just to ask where he was at.

"I'm out with wifey," he replied. "What's up?"

"Sl...Sl...Slim, you know the po..po...po poes is looking for you! They got your picture on all the nn.n.n.news channels.

After listening to Dat finally give him the low down, Tim hung up in disgust. His phone continues to ring from everybody under the sun. Tim couldn't believe how fast the police had gotten on to him. He filled Niecy in on the situation as he paid their bill.

Niecy drove while Tim sat low in the passenger seat. As Niecy drove carefully making sure not to get pulled over, Tim thought about how glad he was that he happened to be out and about when the police raided his home. He knew that if he had been home, the chances were likely he'd either be dead or in jail right now. Niecy pulled up to a motel 8 out on Route 1 in Virginia. She got out by herself and went into the office to rent them a room for the night. As soon as Tim stepped out of the truck he slammed his cell phone on the pavement breaking it into a thousand pieces. Picking up Niecy phone he made an important phone call.

The next morning Tim walked boldly into the Fifth District police station accompanied by his high priced attorney Jennifer Wicks. Jennifer was conservatively dressed in a black Gucci suit, and a pair of Gucci pumps. Hired to the public defender's office straight out of Georgetown University, Jennifer had been one the rising stars. After successfully saving a client from receiving a life sentence for a crime he didn't commit her stocks as a lawyer had risen further. Now in practice for herself, she was considered one of DC's top lawyer hired mouthpieces. While Tim and his lawyer were in the lobby, Detective Stoned and his partner were waiting patiently in the squad room. Detective Stone was the head officer on the Orlean Street murder case. He was tired of getting his ass chewed by the mayor.

"Brown, as soon as we solve this case, I'm taking my ass on vacation." Stone said.

Brown chuckled with a smile on his face. At that moment, he was just glad to be playing second fiddle on this case. He thought back to how hard the captain had been riding his ass when he'd been the lead detective on an eight person shooting that happened as a high school some time back.

At that moment a female officer who'd been manning the front desk, stuck her head in the squad room and asked, "Hey are y'all expecting a Mrs. Wick and Mr. Gamble??"

"Yea, send em on back," Stone said hopping out of his seat like it was on fire.

And the lawyer and her client entered the room Detective Stone approached them with his hand held out. "Good afternoon I'm Detective Stone."

"Hello, my name is Jennifer Wicks, and I am here as Mr. Gamble's attorney. Detective Brown sat quietly watching Tim with his eyes trained to detect even the smallest sign of weakness, but there was none to be found, Tim was cool as a cucumber.

"My client came here voluntarily to answer any questions you might have for him." Jennifer stated.

"That's nice to know, but first I need to frisk Mr. Gamble to see if he has any weapons." Detective Stone said as he stared at Tim with hate filled eyes.

"We don't have a problem with that." Jennifer responded confidently.

After searching Tim, Detective Stone and his partner led them to an interrogation room down the hall. Tim took a seat calmly, appearing as if he didn't have a care in the world.

"We're waiting for an attorney from the USDA's Office." Stone stated. "As soon as she gets here we'll get started."

A few minutes later, a female walked in wearing a Chanel jacket and skirt. As she entered the room she hardly needed an introduction, in fact she was currently prosecuting one of the biggest cases since the Rayful Edmonds trail.

"Hello Jennifer, how are you?" United States District Attorney Phyllis Johnson said with a smile.

"I'm doing fine Phyllis haven't seen you in a while." Jennifer said making small talk.

"How are the husband and kids?"

"Everyone is doing great, thanks for asking." Phyllis replied then looked over to Detective Stone for a reply. She sat down and pulled out a pen and a notepad to take notes. Stones nodded at Detective Brown letting him know that he was ready to begin. Brown immediately pushed the record button on the compact tape recorder he held in his hand.

"Mr. Gamble, I'd like to begin by identifying myself for the record. Stone said,
I'm Detective Stone and I work in the Homicide Unit for the Fifth District. I have a few questions I would like to ask you. Mr. Gamble do you know a man by the name of William Smith?"

"No I don't believe I do!" Tim replied lying through his teeth.

"Maybe you know him by the name Smokey!"

"Nope don't know him either!"

Tim defiant attitude was pissing Stone off, his face turned fire engine red.

"Well I have some on that says differently!" he declared. "So what do you have to say about that?"

"I say that whoever gave you that information, gave you some wrong information!"

"Mr. Gamble, can you tell me where you were two days ago between 8 and 9:00pm?"

"At home fucking my fiancé."

"I'm assuming she's willing to verify that?"

"Ain't no question."

"What's your fiancé name?" Stone asked.

Actually, he already knew the answer to that question, he even knew about the failed kidnapping attempt on her. Unfortunately, he wasn't able to gather enough evidence to arrest Smokey before he was found shot to death, his body lying in some bushes in a wooded area in southeast DC.

"Her name is Denice White." Tim replied.

"Do you have a number for her?"

"Yea, its 202.603.4157."

After a few more bogus questions were asked, Jennifer had had enough,. She knew they didn't have anything on her client the moment they walked in the precinct. If they did Tim would've been cuffed already, not to mention booked in a murder charge.

"Well Detective.." Jennifer said, "Unless you have some new grounds to cover with my client, I believe this interview is over, either charge him with something or we're walking out of here."

Although Stone knew she was only doing her job, it didn't mitigate his angry feeling. "Fucking Bitch!" he thought too "I know she knows his black ass is guilty." While his gut feeling told him that Tim was guilty, Detective Stone knew that he didn't have enough to charge him with anything. A look over at Prosecutor Johnson confirmed that thought.

"I'm not charging him at this moment," Stone said reluctantly. "He's free to go...For now" he added under his breath.

As Sherrill sat in the nail salon, her mind drifted off reminiscing about the last time she'd been there. An unbidden smile crossed her face as she thought about Tim. Since seeing him that last time, she'd been unable to keep him off her mind. She'd tried calling him a few times, but he never answer, she left voicemails, she longed to hear his voice so bad that she would even call just to listen to the short outgoing message on his voicemail. Thinking about it made her want to try again, she pulled her cell phone out and dialed his number. She was so used to his cell going straight to voicemail; that she was shocked to hear him answer on the first ring.

"What's up pretty?" Tim answered in a smooth voice.

"Hey you!" Sherrill responded excitedly. "How you been stranger?"

"Shit I'm good. What you been up to?"

"Just chilling, taking it easy and missing you."

"Is that right?"
"Umm hmm." Sherrill answered smiling through the phone.

"Where you at?" Tim asked.

"I'm at the nail salon in the mall."

Twenty minutes later Sherrill sat on the hood of her Benz waiting for Tim to pull up. It wasn't long before he pulled up in Niecy BMW looking like new money. He was wearing an Armani pin striped suit, a matching Armani shirt and a pair of Ferragamo loafers. Sherrill was smiling from ear to ear as he walked up.

"Hey handsome." she said reaching out for a hug.

Tim hugged her then kissed her on the cheek, causing her pussy to start dripping like a faucet. After looking around the parking lot, he glanced at his watch.

So, Sherrill what did you have planned for the rest of the day?" he asked.

"I was thinking about going to Club Stadium." she replied. "My girlfriend's friends are throwing him a party."

"Oh yea. What's dude name?"

"I don't know, my girlfriend just wanted me to come and party with her. It's supposed to be a private party, if you like I can call my girlfriend and try to get you a pass."

"Naw I'm cool, but I might slide down there later. Me and the owner grew up together so I'll be good."

After hearing Sherrill describe Rome, Tim was glad he'd showed up looking like a legitimate business man. It never paid to let too many people know your business. Tim and Sherrill sat around and talked for a little bit. Although it was really only a few minutes, it seemed like an hour. Tim would have liked to stay longer, but he knew he has to go and meet Tec. He said his goodbyes, and left so he could take a short nap before meeting up with Tec at Club Stadium.

Across Town

Tec sat in his black on black 760 BMW listening to Plies cd The Real Testament. He was parked in front of Ben's Chili Bowl on Florida Avenue waiting on Ebony to show up. A few minutes later Ebony pulled up and parked her Land Rover behind Tec's BMW. Then she got out and joined him in his car. Tec couldn't help but to notice how good she smelled, not to mention, how good she looked in her pair of miss sixty jeans.

"Hey Tec!" she greeted him flashing her bright smile.

"Hey yourself." Tec replied. "How you been doing?"

"I'm better now that I get a chance to spend some time with you, Mr. Man."

"Is that right?" Tec responded with a devilish grin on his face. "So tell me what exactly did you have in mind?"

"I was hoping we could get a room."

"O yea we can do that."

As Tec pulled out of his parking space, Ebony laid back resting her head on the back of the crushed leather seat. Tec raised the volume on his Bose sound system and Trey Songz voice filled the car singing, I bet your neighbors know my name.

"Oh yea," Ebony said with a mischievous grin on her face.

Tec laughed and shook his head.

"Girl you something else."

Twenty minutes later they pulled into the parking lot of the Marriott Hotel in Crystal City, Virginia. They hopped out of the car, walking into to the hotel smiling and grinning like a couple of horny newlyweds. They paid then entered the elevator headed for the penthouse suite. When they entered the room Ebony started rubbing on Tec dick through his jeans, before he even had a chance to turn on the lights. She began unbuttoning his jeans, seconds later they were both butt naked. Ebony was a full figured and curvy woman. She had weight in all the right places, just the way Tec liked it. She was cutter than a bag of good dope.

"I think you're trying to take advantage of me." Tec said in his sexy voice.

Before he could say another word, Ebony kissed him deeply. He tried to speak when she let up, but she silenced him with another kiss. She held him tighter than a white woman holding her purse while walking through the projects at night. Seeing his nine inch uncircumcised penis had her pussy soaking wet. She gazed at him with a lustful look.

"Shit!" Tec exclaimed, "I forgot to get some condoms."

"Didn't expect to get laid on the first night hun?" Ebony asked.

She reached into her purse and pulled out a condom. She tore it open with her teeth, then expertly rolled it onto his rock hard dick. As soon as the condom was on, Ebony laid back on the bed spreading her legs wide, Tec scooted up. Tense and expecting a lot of pain, Ebony was surprised when all she felt was pleasure.

"Gimme that dick!" she yelled at the top of her lungs. Tec gave her just what she asked for, he started humping harder and faster while the sweat rolled down his face.

"Oh yeah" Ebony moaned.

Her pussy was engulfed in a pleasurable kind of pain making her beg for more. Tec grabbed her shoulders pulling her closer. He rammed his dick in and out of her while biting on her neck. Ebony wrapped her legs around his back while he dug in her soaking wet pussy. Ebony was wetter than E-MOTHERFUCKER! Her juices flowed out of her and ran down Tec legs. He tried to hold back, not wanting to cum as he felt his dick exploding like a stick of dynamite.

"Oh hell naw!" she thought to herself.

She had plans on fucking him all night till he fall asleep like a baby. She grabbed his dick and examine it like she was a doctor. She stroked it until it got hard again then jammed it into her mouth. She began slurping on his dick until it was completely coated with her saliva. When she began taking small sucks the intensity drove him crazy. Seconds later his dick erupted like a volcano in her mouth filling it with semen. Tec fell back feeling weaker than superman around kryptonite. They laid on the bed, their bodies glued together as they fell asleep.

Niecy pulled Tim's corvette into the driveway, and parked next to her X5. She spent most of her morning at the DMV renewing Tim's tags. She planned on taking a shower and going to sleep. She walked over to her truck to grab her new Anthony Hamilton cd before going in the house. She used the remote on her key ring to disarm her car alarm before getting in. As she grabbed the CD she noticed Tim's cell phone sitting on the seat. Usually she wouldn't even touch his phone, but her curiosity got the better of her. She picked the phone up, flipped it open and began thumbing through the menu. He had a new text message she read it: Tim it was nice seeing you. I thought you didn't want to see me again, ever since we spent that night together I haven't been the same. I've been thinking about you 24/7 and missing you. Sherrill.

Niecy was beyond angry. She couldn't take it anymore. The worrying about him at night, the looking the other way as if she didn't notice things a blind person could see, she had enough. She always tried to justify Tim actions, but she was through making excuses for him. Hearing another woman saying she missed him broke her heart, not to mention their trust. She stormed into the house headed straight to the bedroom. Tim was laid up in the bed between some silk polo sheets. He opened his eyes to find Niecy standing over him. She was staring at him with a crazy look in her eyes. He could feel the tension in the air.

"Wow here we go again." he thought to himself.

"Tim who the fuck is Sherrill?!" Niecy asked with an attitude.

She stood with her hands on her hips waiting for an answer, like a crackhead asking for credit. "Who" Tim asked feigning ignorance.

"Sherrill mu fucker!" Niecy said with her eyes trained on him like an FBI agent in surveillance.

"Sh..she ain't nobody."

"Then if she ain't nobody why in the fuck is she texting you talking about she miss you!"

Tim face told it all. He badly wanted to come clean after seeing the hurt expression on her face. He took a deep breath, then let it out slowly. He still couldn't find the courage to answer.

"You know what lover, don't even worry about it." Niecy finally said before walking out.

Tec phones vibrated as it lay on the hotel night stand, glancing over and seeing Ebony wasn't in the room, he picked it up and answered it.

"Hello"

"Where you at slim?" Tim asked

"Shit my bad slim." Tec said looking at his watch, give me thirty minutes."

Once Tim arrived to Club Stadium, he pulled into the valet parking lot. He scanned the parking lot looking for Tec BMW, but didn't see it. As he was about to call Tec cell a white 420 Mercedes pulled up behind him with the high beams damn near blinding him. He got out of his car, paid the valet worker, and then looked at the Mercedes.

"What's up Tim?" the driver asked

"What's up Tyini Boo?"

"That's what I'm trying to find out." she shot back.

A chuckle escaped Tim mouth as he replied. "Come on Tyini either we gonna carry it like brother and sister or we gonna carry it like lovers."

"Tim I'm tired of playing this brother and sister shit." Tyini said. "You know damn well you want to fuck me, so what's up, when you going to give me some of that dick?"

"Tyini you know you are fine as E MOTHERFUCKER, and ain't no question I've definitely thought about hitting that, but let's keep it real, if we start fucking not its only gonna fuck up our friendship."

"Yeah right, you just know that once you hit this good pussy you gonna wanna keep hitting it every chance you get." She responded punching him playfully on the arm.

"True...True...True.." Tim said with a goofy smile on his face.

"Okay Tim, I 'ma holla at you, I gotta go over there and holla at my girls." she said.

Tyini sashayed over to the rest of the Hechinger Mall honeys: Pepper, Sexy Ann, Lisa of the world Peasley and Super Duper Cooper. They all were looking radiant. Tim looked up and saw Sherrill walk into the club. He let out a sigh hypnotized by her beauty. He casually walked up behind her. The music was loud. All of the top money getters were there. There were all different types of money getters even Pimps Ju Ju and Don Juan and a few of their whores showed up. Dat and the Potomac Gardens crew, Stan Hunt and his little cousins Ray Ray, Fat Trey, 21 Street Pie, Steve Omar Bush, Jack and the M Street Crew Pinball, Joe Black, Tae, Mal, Gooch, Cricket and Football showed up for the gathering.

After seeing all the crews in attendance, Tim thought about Tec and his cousin Mike, "I miss you Mike he said looking up in the air." He pulled out his cell and dialed Tec, but it went straight to voicemail. Even with the flashing strobe lights, he spotted Sherrill standing by the bar. She was wearing a Prada dress with the back out. Along with a matching purse and a pair of stilettos. Her shoulder length dreads looked freshly done. Tim looked her over from head to toe, then crept up silently behind her.

"Hello beautiful." he whispered in her ear.

Sherrill turned around with that million dollar smile on her face.

"What you smiling for?" Tim asked.

"I'm smiling because I'm happy to see you." She answered.

Tim pulled her close and started kissing and sucking on her lips.

"Boy don't start nothing you can't finish." Sherrill warned.

Tim didn't respond, he continued kissing her long and passionately, not caring who saw them.

"All that money you got, Ni...Ni...Nigga get a room!" Someone said.

Tim turned around to find Dat standing behind him smiling.

"Sherrill turned up her nose and rolled her eyes. Tim felt a bad vibe as he notice Sherrill attitude drastically change.

"Sherrill, I..I..I.. know you ain't still tripping about that shit at the Zanzibar." Dat stuttered.

"You damn right I am." Sherrill snapped. "You thought that foul ass shit was cute."

"Damn boo that shit was over a year ago."

"Tim I'll see you later." Sherrill said ignoring Dat. "I'm going to go check on my girlfriend."

She kissed his lips, then strutted over to the VIP section. Tim couldn't wait to find out what had happened between Sherrill and Dat.

"What was that all about?" Tim asked knowing that Dat was always saying and doing some wild ass shit.

"Slim, one night I was at the club and Sherrill and her friend was in there." Dat explained. "So I let them sit at my table. After the bitch Lee started drinking up m..m...my shit, I asked the bitch for some head. Then the bi..bi..bitch got an attitude. So I had security throw the hoes out the club."

Tim just shook his head. "Nigga you outta line." Tim said with a smile on his face.

"Fuck that shit slim." Dat said. "Your m..man R..R...Rome in the VIP getting his freak on.

"Oh yeah!"

"Slim I 'ma go to the r..r..restroom, and I'll meet you back there."

"Cool." Tim said shaking Dat hand before walking into the VIP Room.

Rome was feeling good. He has a bottle of Cristal in one hand and a blunt in the other, while a female sat in his lap. Tim looked at him in shock. Rome was oblivious, his face showing pleasure as the girl grinded harder on his lap.

"You like this don't you?" the girl asked as she felt his dick on her ass poking through his penis.

Rome's voice was slurred as he answered, "hell yea," he said while squeezing on her breasts.

"You better not let Trina hear you say that!" Tim teased.

"What's up Tim?" Curly greeted him with a bear hug. "I've been waiting on you to show up."

Curly was the owner of Club Stadium back in the day before he went legit. Curly had his hand in a little bit of everything. He was well known and respected throughout the city. A man always immaculately dressed, people called him Curly because of the texture of his hair. He was soft spoken, but when he did speak, everyone around him listened.

"Tim I got a few things I need to take care of." Curly said, "But I'll make sure you have everything you need, and it's all on the house.

"I appreciate that Curly, but I'm good."

"Nigga how many times do I have to tell you that when you're in here your money's no good!"

A few minutes later a waitress and a bouncer walked up carrying two bottles of Belvedere, two bottle of Moet, a gallon of VSOP Remy, two bottles of Cîroc and four bottles of Patron.

"This is courtesy of the club." the waitress said with a smile.

Tim reached in his pocket and pulled out a big wad of bills so he could give her a tip. However, she waved him off.

"What's wrong sweetie?" Tim asked, "I'm just trying to give you a little something for your service."

"Thanks but no thanks. The owner already took care of everything."

"Well can you do me a favor?" Tim asked as he grabbed a bottle of Moet. "Take this and give it to the young lady over there." he said pointing at Sherrill.

"I sure can."

Sherrill was sitting at a small table waiting on Lee. Her dreadlocks swayed back and forth as she bobbed her head back and forth to the beat of the music.

"Here this is for you, compliments of the gentleman over there." the waitress said pointing over at Tim.

Sherrill looked over and saw Tim smiling at her. He blew her a kiss and waved her over. On her way over Cricket who was drunk out of his mind, spoke to her. "What it do boo?"

"You trying to do something for two something?" Cricket asked grabbing her arm.

"Nigga you got me fucked up!" she said jerking her arm away.

"Naw bitch, you been fucked up with ya raggedy ass," Cricket shouted while his crew laughed like he said the funniest joke ever.

"Fuck you bitch ass nigga!"

"What you say to me bitch?" Cricket said feeling disrespected.

"You heard me motherfucker!"

When Tim looked over and saw the way Cricket was swole up in Sherrill face he rushed over. Cricket took a step towards Sherrill, looking like he was about to slap her. "You got a problem?" Tim asked with a menacing look on his face. Cricket turned around to see Tim staring him down. Out of nowhere, Tec came and stood beside Tim, his eye locked on Cricket. As bad as he wanted to slap the shit out of Sherrill, Cricket didn't want to start a war he wasn't capable of ending.

"Naw we ain't got no problem." Cricket said with a smirk.

"That's what I thought." Tim said as he draped his arm around Sherrill and kissed her on the cheek. Tim never liked Cricket, on any other night he would've been trying to beat the brakes off of him. He just didn't wanna ruin Rome's night. He made a mental note in his head to deal with Cricket later in a deadly way.

"You okay?" Tim asked Sherrill smiling at the way she'd went head to head with a man twice her size.

"Yea I'm good."

Tim and Sherrill walked off headed in the direction of Rome's table, while Tec trailed behind them with a devilish smirk on his face.

The club screamed their approval, as the DJ shouted welcome home Rome on the microphone. For his part Rome seemed to be having the time of his life. Usually the laid back type. The time he spent in jail, had him acting out of character, standing on a table, surrounded by Dat and his crew and plenty of strippers. Rome had a bottle of Moet in each hand dousing the crowd with frothy champagne making it rain literally. Once the trio arrived at Rome table, Lee was grinding up on Rome swaying to the music. Rome dick was harder than a jaw breaker, Grabbing Sherrill hand Tim looked at Tec, then nodded his head, letting him know that everything was cool.

As player circle song Duffle Bag Boy came blasting out the club speaker, Tim smiled and pulled Sherrill onto the dance floor. She wrapped her arms around his waist and began rocking her hips, Tim gripped both of Sherrill ass cheeks as he rocked with her back and forth. The entire clubs attention was on the pair as they danced together having a good time. Out of the corner of his eyes, Tim caught a glimpse of the Hechinger Mall honeys staring at them. Tyini Boo was astonished by the way he was all up in Sherrill face dancing and acting like he was having a ball. Making sure Tim saw her, Tyini boo dropped down and started bouncing her ass like a Chevy hitting switches. He just shook his head and continued getting his groove on. Tec was happy to see his partner enjoying himself. The party began to wind down around 2:30 in the morning. As the people started leaving the club, Jack walked over with a worried look in his face. Tim was sitting down having a conversation with Sherrill. Rome was also sitting with them inhaling weed smoke. Lee was in his face like make up. Jack eased between the crowd.

"Tim let me holla at you for a minute." Jack insisted.

"What's up slim?" Tim asked checking for a reaction knowing he was aware of the situation between him and Cricket. Speaking over the loud music.

"Tim looked over to Sherrill before stepping off. "Sherrill excuse me for a minute, lemme holla at my man real quick."

"Alright." Sherrill replied happy to see how Tim respected her presence. When she peered over and seen how Lee was grinding over Rome. Suddenly she reflected to all the freaky stories she'd heard about Lee. She locked her attention back to Tim wondering what they were talking about. ....

When Tim and Jack were out of eyeshot, Tim spoke first.

"What's up Jack?"

"Slim Cricket told me y'all had words. Slim he didn't want no problem with you, he didn't know ole girl was your people." Jack tried his hardest to defuse the situation.

Tim face twisted up instantly with every word Jack spoke.
"Man, I'm not trying to hear that shit!" Tim raised his voice. "It's on sight when I see that nigga. He's a dead man!"

"Come on slim." Jack pleaded. "He was drunk and he don't want no smoke with you."

He was fucking with Jack and Tim was trying his hardest to hold his laughter, getting a kick out of his reaction. A smile finally broke, and Jack realized he was the butt of the joke.

"Nigga…. Why you always on some bullshit." Jack asked as he joined the laughter.

"Slim you should have seen your face." Tim said still laughing at Jack. "Naw slim I'm not tripping off the nigger, he straightened his face showing his seriousness."

"As long as he stay in his lane and don't get outta pocket no more."

Jack nodded his head seeing how serious Tim was, but he understood. Inside Jack was relieved that the situation was minor and could be handled in that fashion, Lord knows things could have gotten ugly. Seeing how empty the club was Tim decided he was ready to leave. After he said his goodbyes he approached the table where Sherrill sat, all while Rome and Lee were still glued to one another. Sherrill leaned in before she spoke, "Look like I'm gonna need a ride home." Referring to Rome and Lee sex-scapade.

Tim cracked a smile, "You know I got you shawdy."

After Tim pulled up on Rome and told him to be safe they promised to hook up the following morning. Sherrill and Tim casually exited the club. Tim stayed a few steps behind her slightly mesmerized by the sway of her hips. Sherrill knew Tim was watching, so she put an extra strut in her step. After a short ride Tim pulled into the front of Sherrill spot. She seductively licked her lips when she asked, "you wanna come up?"

Visions of Niecy face appeared, and he knew how she reacted the last time he let the sun beat him home. Tim took a deep breath. "I'll pass, tonight not a good night." It hurt him to say that.

With a look of disappointment she replied, "I understand."

She stared at the bulge in his pants which made her mouth water. She was horny, hot and bothered. Even though Tim declined her offer he didn't say no. She went for what she knew. She reached over and gripped his dick through his pants. Tim put up no resistance.

"Let me suck that dick!" She eased closer while moving the middle console. Tim lifted his hips as he unzip his pants. Once his dick was fully exposed, Sherrill wasted no time going to work. She worked her head back and forth, up and down, then fast and slow. The slurping sounds mixed with the wetness of her mouth drove him crazy. He pressed his head against the headrest, tilted his seat back and grabbed a handful of her dreads….

When Niecy opened her eyes, she rolled over to yet another empty space. She peered over at the digital clock which read 4:05am.

"This nigga got me fucked up." she mumbled to herself feeling like Tim was losing respect for her and their relationship. She decided to get up headed over to her huge walk-in closet. She hit the light switch, looking around, she noticed all the designer coats, furs, boots, bags, belts, Gucci, Prada, Moi-Moi, and all the things she ever wanted. Tears streamed down her pretty cheeks as thoughts of giving all her shit away just to have a man that loves and wants to be with her.

She knelt down and removed some boxes, until she was face to face with Tim safe. She entered the code not missing a beat and the lock unlatched. She stared at all the neatly stacked hundred dollar bills. She grabbed her Gucci bag, and tossed two the stacked bills in her purse, then closed it back. She walked over to her laptop then logged on to www.travelagent.com. Moments later she was given a confirmation number for a first class roundtrip flight to Jamaica. She then pulled up another site, and booked a private villa in Round Hill Resort located in Montego Bay. Quickly she packed a week and a half worth of clothes into her Louis Vuitton suitcase.

Knowing time was of the essence she didn't want to get caught in the act. She dragged her luggage to their living room closet and stashed it. She made it her business to leave the computer on so he could see the reservation she made and it would be too late to stop her. She heard the car pulling up in the driveway and instantly knew it was Tim. Killing the engine he looked at his beautiful home. As he looked around he noticed all the lights in the house were off besides the living room. He gripped his pistol keeping it out as he walked towards his home. When he entered his house, the first thing he saw was Niecy sitting on the couch with an attitude written all over her face.

"I see you remember where you live." Niecy spoke with pure sarcasm.

Tim took a deep breath, not really wanting to be bothered with her bullshit. Choosing not to respond he made his way toward the kitchen.

"Them stinky ass bitches are going to be your downfall Tim."

Unable to let it slide, Tim spun around on his heels, "why every time you get mad about something? Or I don't come home in a time you want me to, I gotta be with another bitch?" he let those words sink in.

"That's some insecure shit."

Niecy wore a devilish smirk as she crossed her legs. "Don't even worry about it...I'm good."

With that being said she stood to her feet and headed toward their bedroom.

The next morning Niecy was up bright and early while Tim was knocked out sleep. For some reason he was sleep with a smile on his face.

"Yeah smile now I'll be the one laughing later on." she mumbled.

As much as she wanted to stab him repeatedly she held her composure. Instead she went downstairs and dressed quietly. Putting on her mo-moi sweat suit and Prada sneakers she'd hidden in the closet along with her luggage. After she was done she sat down to write Tim a letter.

Dear Tim,

I love you and you know this. If I don't leave now I'm going to do something I would regret. I really feel like hurting you, but hurting you would be like hurting myself. And I love myself enough to know we need a break. If you love something let it go, if it come back it was meant to be.

Love,

Niecy

When she was done writing the letter she grabbed her purse and luggage. After she taped the letter to the front door, she walked out the house. She loaded everything into the truck then headed to the airport.

An Hour Later

Niecy sat in a plush first class seat looking out the windows staring at the Ronald Reagan National Airport. She thought about picking up her cell phone and calling Tim, but the thought of him pleasing another woman haunted her vision. "Fucking nigga" she thought.

As the flight attendant approached with a smile on her face. Niecy smiled as well.

"May I have a double shot of patron please?" Niecy eyed the long legged blonde knowing exactly why these airlines hired these young women. After taking the drink to the head, Niecy leaned back in her seat then prepared for takeoff…….

Six Hours Later

Niecy strutted her way through Montego Bay Airport. She turned the heads of men and women as she stepped into the humid air. The temperature had to be in the high hundreds, and the sun was beaning off her honey bronze skin. Niecy scanned the waiting area until she spotted her name in large letters. As she approached she noticed just how attractive the man who was holding the sign with her name on it was. She seized him up from his relaxed sandals, cargo shorts and a half button shirt that did not do a good job hiding his muscular frame.

"Damn he fine" she thought as she licked her lips. She felt a surge of moisture flow to her pussy. Wearing her jogging suit open exposing enough cleavage to stop traffic. Adjusting her cleavage the closer she got the sexier he became.

"Hello Madam, welcome to Jamaica." he spoke with a strong Jamaican accent.

"Hey" she shot back not able to speak a full sentence.

"Malcom," he said extending his large hand.

The sexual attraction between the two was obvious, he stared at her matching her stare, for a second it seemed as if time stopped and it was just the two of them outside the airport. Thoughts of watching him licking and sucking on her clit crossed her mind, the bulge in his pants made her envision herself on her knees giving him the best head he'd ever had, snapping out of her daze she asked, "So how long will it take to get to the resort?" Making small talk trying to break the tension.

"About a twenty minute ride" he said as he grabbed the luggage from her hands, the slight touch from his hands sent chills up her spine.

"We should get going" she said basically throwing her ass from side to side giving him a full shot of her backside. The driver smiled at the sight before him. He was used to women from the states throwing themselves at the Jamaican men.

Especially when they were by themselves, or in a group. He knew the saying was true what happens in Jamaica stays in Jamaica.

Niecy sat in the back of the limo flushing with thoughts of the mysterious driver. As much as she wanted to get Tim back by giving the driver some pussy, she couldn't bring herself to doing it. She knew her and Tim would never leave one another that was her truth. She let the window down and enjoyed the view. "I can't fuck him, but I might suck his dick if he plays his cards right."

It was 1:32pm when Tim woke up and glanced at the clock on the nightstand. The feeling of a nerve wrecking headache sat overtop his left eye. He sat up and headed to the bathroom. After he relieved himself he searched his medicine cabinet for some Tylenols. Walking back to the bathroom he called Niecy but received no answer. He looked out the window and noticed Niecy truck was missing.

He picked up his cellphone and dialed Niecy's cell, it went straight to voicemail. He tried once more before he decided to get dressed and make some runs. After he showered he was heading towards the door, that's when he noticed a piece of paper taped to the door. He grabbed it and opened it, after reading the contents he grew angry, bitter, hurt and most important jealous. Never in a million years did he think she would just up and leave.

Thoughts of her being with another man bruised his ego and tore at his heart.

"Snap out of it Tim" he thought trying to put on his I don't give a fuck attitude.

"Maybe she just needed a massage or something, she'll be back." As he pushed the door open then walked out and locked up he hopped in his vette. As he pushed down the highway all sorts of thoughts and visions of Niecy with another man crossed his mind. He was so caught up in his conscious that when he looked down at the dashboard he was doing 149mph. With all the things going on in his head, going to jail wasn't part of his plan. If it was anybody who knew where Niecy was, it would be Trina. He picked up his phone and dialed her number.

"Hello" she answered on the second ring.

"What's up Trina, have you seen my baby? A nigga sick over this mufucker." he laughed but meant every word.

She laughed along with him. "Yeah we talked right before she got on her flight."

"What flight?...To where? He raised his voice.

"She needed to get away for a while she said."

"Where is she? He got more upset as he spoke.

Trina didn't respond right away, instead she just laughed.

"What's so damn funny?"
"I'm sorry Tim" she stopped laughing. Niecy said you would be calling that's all. She did tell me to tell you if you can come join her at the Round Hill Resort in Montego Bay, Jamaica."

Feeling like there was nothing else to be said he hung up. "I wish the fuck I would" he said out loud as he exited the highway and headed back home. He was pissed and contemplated on calling a moving company to pack all Niecy shit and take it to storage, or better yet the goodwill. He wanted to leave Niecy, but deep down he knew it would never happen. He called her cell phone once more and it went straight to voicemail. His mind was playing tricks on him, and the saying was true, "It ain't no fun when the rabbit got the gun." He sat down at the computer preparing to log on when he moved the mouse, Niecy itinerary popped up on the screen. "BINGO!" he busted out. He cracked a smile as he googled a flower shop near Round Hill Resort. Once he located one he dialed the number instantly.

Niecy ass naked sat down in the bubbling jacuzzi the scent of Paris Hilton Black bath oil gave off the sexiest scent thus putting her in the mood. She took another sip of her patron them laid her head back to enjoy the jacuzzi jets. Before she knew it she found her two fingers massaging her clit. In a circular motion she closed her eyes and thought the limo driver. She envisioned them in a 69 position. She held his dick in her throat while savoring the taste of his nut. She sucked and slurped while he exploded in her mouth. Her knees buckled as her orgasm was finding its way through her spine. She was about to nut, then suddenly knock, knock, knock someone knocked on the villa door.

"Oh shit" she jumped, startled then opened her eyes. "Umm hold on!' she called out "maybe it's him." She put on a silk sexy robe with nothing under while her body still glistened with water. She opened the door to see a woman holding a bouquet of flowers.

"Delivery for Ms. White," she smiled while she gave Niecy a once over.

"Yes that's me, thank you." Niecy said accepting the flowers then quickly reading the card just assure they were from the limo man.

The things I would give up for there to be another us. I would give up my left eye, even give up my style just to keep my right eye just so I could see your smile, I would give up my left hand, but keep the right just so I could feel the tenderness of your hand. You already have my soul, so why leave me in the cold. Without you in my world I'm all alone and messed up. I need you baby and I'm sorry. You never know what you have till it's gone, but you never know what you had unless you know it's worth. Love Tim

Tears began to fall from her eyes, she felt overwhelmed with love and joy. That quick she fell back in love with him. The real Tim she'd fell for years ago. Beyond the surface she felt dirty and wrong. Here it is she has a man who loves her period drawers and she playing with herself thinking about the next nigga. She kissed the card and whispered, "I love you Tim."

Niecy couldn't control her guilt; she felt like shit, she felt as if she'd cheated on him by playing with herself while thinking about another man. Feeling stuck between a rock and a hard spot, she did what her heart told her to so. She packed her bags and decided she wanted to be with her man... After booking a flight back home for 3:00pm that evening she decided to have a drank to ease the emotions that were running through her. As she exited the villa and made her way to a nearby restaurant, she felt someone close behind her. When she looked over her shoulders there stood Malcolm the limo driver. Niecy not only was lost for words, but she lost her thoughts.

"Hello Madam." he spoke flashing his pearly whites.

"Hey...y..you!" she stuttered before he could get another word out. She closed the distance between them taking control over the situation. The six-inch Lesare Paciotto Bontoni high heel sandals she wore had her standing eye to eye with him.

"I'm going to be honest with you." she paused taking in the romantic scenery around her, a cool breeze, shining sun and fairly empty streets. "I'm gonna begin by telling you that I'm in love with my man, he's good to me... It's just at times I don't understand him. He loves me and I love him." She peeked down at the bulge in his linen shorts. "Under any different any different circumstances I'll be riding you till the sun came up."

He pulled her closer by the small of her back bringing his lips within inches of hers. Their breath met in pace. "You love him? He asked and she nodded. "Then go to him and fight for what you want, give him all of your love and don't take no for an answer." With that said, she turned around and walked away.

When Niecy finally reached home, she was taken away by the car that occupied her spot. "What the fuck?: she thought as she slammed her truck in park and jumped out to take a closer look at the vehicle. There sat a brand new pink Bentley GT coupe with 22 inch rims with paper tags. She ran her mental rolodex to what bitch in the hood had a pink Bentley. She ran up the stairs and fumbled with her keys till she opened the door. The sounds of Carl Thomas Emotional blared through the speakers coming from the bedroom. Like the DEA on a drug raid The first thing she saw Tim was playing with himself. She looked around the room and ran straight to the bathroom. She came back out the opened the closet door then looked under the bed.

"Tim!" Whose car is that in my parking spot?" she barked feeling stupid for rushing home to the bullshit.

"What car?" Tim asked not looking in her direction.

"Bitch you know what car I'm talking about! You no good muhfucker!"

"Niecy what are you talking about?"

"I flew back to get home to you, and you got a bitch in our fucking home Tim! I fucking hate you nigga!" she screamed as tears began to form in her eyes.

"You don't hate me." Tim said calm with a smile on his face.

"Oh.. You think this a game nigga? I'm leaving your bitch ass nigga." She turned around to walk off. Tim grabbed her and hugged her tight.

"Get off me!" she yelled trying to fight him.

"Not until you hear me out!" he shouted then let her go.

He ran behind her all the way out the door. Niecy was so upset she went to the trunk of her X5 to grab the handle to the jack to fix a flat, she was about to bust the window, till Tim hit the alarm, bringing the car to life. She stopped dead in her tracks, as Tim opened the passenger door and pulled out a small plastic bag. Niecy was confused, hurt and more confused.

"I go out and buy you a hundred thousand dollar whip, and this is the type of thanks I get."

He handed her the bill of sale. She looked down and seen her name on the dotted line, a smile crossed her cheeks.

"Maybe I should have gotten it in black." he smiled and opened his arms. Like a little girl missing her father, she ran to him and jumped in his arm.

"Tim I'm so embarrassed, I'm so sorry."

The weather was in the high eighties and everybody and their mama's was out enjoying the heat. Trina boo and the Hechinger mall honeys were out wearing low cut booty shorts, skirts, an open toe sandals. While the fellas showed off their tattoos, Solbiato sweat suits, Hugo boss short sets and the latest 993 new balance. The streets were so packed you would have thought Jay Z was having a conversation.

"Damn slim" Rell paused and took in the scenery around him. "Y'all got this block wide the fuck open."

"Yeah slim, that comes from having that good shit, the product gonna speak for itself" he boasted while thinking about the money he was going to bring in..

"What I need to get in?"

Black Tae knew where this conversation was going, he'd rather Rell play his position.

"Slim you a good nigga, stick to the murder game, that's what you good at?" he paused then reminisced a few years back.

"Rell! Remember when we first met in juvie? You sold that cop a bag of weed. He laughed to himself. Your dumb ass was on a school trip to

195

the White House and you selling weed. He continued to laugh, dumb nigga there."

Rell couldn't help but to laugh as well. "Yea you right." Rell said thinking back to that day. They both enjoyed the moment. Rell and Black Tae continued their conversation till Cricket walked up with a facial expression screwed up.

"What's good?" Tae asked "is everything good my nigga!"

Rell nodded his head in Cricket direction, he instantly picked up on the vibe from the look on Cricket face.

"Naw slim, that nigga Tim and his man Tec got me fucked up." Cricket said still with an attitude.

Tae stared at him not wanting to hear it.

"Man go head with that bullshit!" Tae knew Cricket was dealing with his emotions, he always got himself into shit that he couldn't handle.

Cricket took a deep breath then sucked his teeth. "Slim them niggas ain't the only one with guns." he said .pulling up his shirt revealing the 45 magnum on his waist.

"So you a killer now?" Black Tae said looking him up and down.

"You better be, because them niggas don't be playing no games, so if you go at them, go hard, or fall the fuck back!"

"Cricket stood silent.....Yea I hear ya!"

Rell looked on not caring how he played it, if Tim gave him the word Cricket would be dead where he stood.

"What's up Rell? Tim asked

"Slim I need to holla at you about something I just heard."

Tim peered over and looked at Niecy who was standing next to her new Bentley Coupe, waiting to take it for a spin. She was smiling like a kid on Christmas day.

"Where you wanna meet?" Tim asked still staring at Niecy.

"You tell me."

"Okay, meet me at Iverson Mall in thirty minutes."

"Bet." Rell said before ending the call.

Niecy was pushing the coupe like Dana Patrick. She was racing the engine to 120 mph, while Tim smiled. It made him happy to see her smiling, especially with all the pain he'd caused her. He thought back to the last time he'd seen her happy, then he became upset. "She shouldn't only be happy during sex, I want to make her happy all the time." The car slowed down approaching the mall parking lot.

Rell sat in front of Cameron's Seafood in Iverson Mall parking lot, he stared at the Bentley. Damn that got to be a bad ass bitch pushing that motherfucker..... He thought to himself.

The Bentley pulled beside his cocaine white Range Rover. He just smiled with the thought of putting his mack down. Tim hopped out the passenger side smiling at his little conrad. Rell was speechless after seeing him getting out.

"What's up my nigga?" Tim said punching his fist out for some dap. Rell dapped him. "Slim I was on M Street and that pussy nigga Cricket was pulling his pistol out running his mouth talking some fake ass tough shit like he was trying to see you."

"O yea!" Tim said with a grin on his face.

"Slim give me the word, it ain't in the talk and I push that faggot hairline back. Kill moe on everything I love."

"Hit me when it's done."

Tec opened his eyes and cracked a smile when he saw Ebony. It's been a long time since he spent quality time with a woman. After seeing how his mother betrayed his father his motto was "fuck em and let em fry!" But there was something about Ebony that seemed different. It felt right. He reached his arm around her and pulled her in for a kiss. Once their lips intertwined he began to fondle her breast. His lips moved from her lips to her neck. He was dying to slide his dick inside of her.

When he rose up dick harder than the neighborhood he grew up in, Ebony took one look then went to work. She wrapped her lips around the shaft then kissed the head before making it disappear before his eyes. Seeing the bulge in her throat along with a mouth full of spit he was instantly in love. She held that position causing his knees to get weak. She sucked him slow while she stared him deep in his eyes. He felt his dick pulsate in her mouth so she went down a lil deeper as he bust nut in her mouth. She continued to suck every drop until it was completely gone...

"Got damn it!" He sighed before he leaned over and kissed her forehead. "Damn... you like that shawdy." His chest heaved up and down as he imitated Red Foxx. "I'm coming to join you honey."

They both shared a laugh before staring at each other.

Tec stood to his feet, still wobbly from the mind blowing head he just received moments ago. He made his way to the shower with thoughts of a sexy evening he'd planned for Ebony. They were gonna go to Georgetown to have brunch on a private boat, and sail down the shore course lake.

"Damn I'm getting soft as shit." he thought to himself as he stepped in the shower.

Fifteen Minutes Later

Tec came out the shower drying off when he locked eyes with Ebony. It took him a moment to realize what she had in her hand. She had a gun pointed at him. He tensed up then froze in his tracks.

"Bitch!"

"Shut the fuck up!" she shouted, cutting him off while the gun trembled in her hands. He took a step forward.

"Move again and I'll blow your fucking brains out!" By now tears mixed with sweat poured down her pretty face, her look was serious and the grip she had on the Beretta 9mm showed she was serious.

"You remember Duke and Darrell motherfucker!" She raised her voice "They were my brothers and you killed them!" She used her free hand to wipe her face and held her aim at his midsection.

Never in Tec's wildest dream did he imagine being caught slipping, literally with his pants down by a bitch he fell for. Deciding to try his hand, he attempted to lunge at her. She squeezed the trigger five times POP.POP.POP.POP.POP Ebony emptied the clip in Tec, in panic she fled the scene dropping the gun in the process, leaving Tec to die in a puddle of his own blood.

Niecy was so into the words of Sade "Is it a crime", that she didn't notice she was doing 80 mph in a 65 mph zone. She loved the way the Bentley Coupe hugged the road and rove so smooth. Not to mention the 16 speaker Bose sound system to put the icing on the cake. Tim smiled at the sign of her happiness. Playing the passenger side he couldn't help but caress Niecy's thighs. She wore a Vera Wang mini dress with a 6 inch pair of Giuseppe Zand, lace up heels. The sight of all her cleavage made him want to taste her.

(VRRRR.VRRRR)

The vibration on his hip alarmed him of an incoming call. He noticed Rosedale Rell number.

Knowing what this call may be about he quickly answered.

"What's good playboy?" Tim spoke into the phone.

"Slim you see the news?"

Tim knew it couldn't be good. "Naw, I'm on the highway, what's up?"

Rell took a deep breath. "Tec dead, he paused letting his words sink in also becoming emotional. Slim they found him in a hotel."

"What!" Tim yelled into the phone, startling Niecy.

"Slim they locked Duke and Darrell sister up for the murder."

"Shit!" Tim smashed his cell phone into the dashboard, shattering it to pieces.

Niecy looked over in shock. In panic she slammed on the brakes. Once coming to a complete stop on the shoulder she asked, "baby what's wrong?"

By now tears were falling from his face. The thought of his best friend being murdered felt like a knife was in his chest.

"Turn this motherfucker around!"

"Baby what's wrong? She placed both her hands on his face.

"Tec...Tec Dead!"

Sherrill inhaled deep on her Newport long, she sat in a parked rental car in Bowie, Maryland. From behind the tints of the Magnum. She carefully loaded bullets in the snub nose 38. "There you go" she whispered finally seeing her mark. She'd sat and waited for hours for this moment, and she would not fuck this up. She took a deep breath then exited the car. She pulled her black north face hoodie over her head and approached her prey. Hearing the footsteps behind him quickly he spun around.

The last thing he heard was the sound of the revolver being cocked back. When he finally adjusted his eyes all he saw was the sparks. Boom..Boom..Boom..Boom..! The bullets crashed into his chest knocking him back against the car. He was still standing on his feet. He held his chest and looked up. Seeing this she continued to choke the trigger until there were no bullets left. He fell to the ground his body went into convulsions. She reached into her coat pocket and pulled out a K-bar 6 inch army knife. She stood over him, looked around and slit his throat, then stabbed him in the heart.

"You picked the wrong bitch to fuck with!" she said leaving Cricket in a puddle of his own blood.

"What do you think partner?" Detective Stone asked his partner Detective Brown as they stood over Tec's dead body. He was shot repeatedly. Detective Stone and Brown were notified by Virginia Eastern Homicide District. They were told they had a man identified as Delone Kerry. They rushed to the crime scene immediately which was the Marriott Hotel. When they arrived the lead detective pulled the white sheet back and exposed the face of one of the ruthless killers known on the DC streets as Tec.

Ever since Tim got the call about Tec's death his mind has been playing tricks on him. Everything from homicidal thoughts to hearing Tec's voice in his head. The pain he felt at this very moment was similar to how he felt when his brother died. He wanted revenge as he contemplated on how he was gonna kill the bitch responsible for his grief, had him thinking reckless. He didn't care who had to go. If anybody got in the way they would be dealt with.

Niecy turned the Bentley around and headed back to DC moments later she pulled up to Tec mother's house. Tim wiped the tears from his eyes with the back of his hand, then got himself together. He hated being the bearer of bad news, but he knew Tec would do it for him. Together he and Niecy walked to the same apartment building where he and Tec became friends. Tim was hesitant as he knocked on the door. Ms. Kerry opened the door. Her eyes puffy and red. Matching Tim's exactly. Tim reached out to grab her hand, attempting to ease the situation. Showing sympathy... She snatched her hand away.

"Tim is my child alive?" she asked straightforward.

It took all the strength he had, "no ma'am."

She stared deep into Tim's eyes. She'd always told Tec the streets that he loved so much, would kill him. She wasn't prepared for this day to actually come.

One Week Later

Ever since Tec death, Tim drank more, smoked more and slept less. He was losing weight drastically, Niecy stood by his side. She begged him to go get himself out the slump he was in. She did her best to stay strong for the both of them. She knelt down next to him while he laid in the bed. She kissed his forehead, then placed in his hand a card she bought while she was out running errands. When Tim heard the door close, he opened his teary eyes and opened the card. It read, "I know you been through so much lately and I know it's taken a lot out of you and at times it may seem like things will never be normal again. But I know you'll handle it. You're one of the bravest people I've ever known, you might not see it that way but I do. You have an inner strength that keeps you hanging on in situations that would try the best of us. That's not to say that the day and weeks ahead that you need someone to remind you just how wonderful you are. I'm here. Love Niecy...

"Niecy!" he yelled to the top of his lungs. Jumping out the bed he reached for the fifth of XO Remy. He threw it with all his might to the wall. Causing the glass to shatter and pictures fell from the walls.

Niecy heard the commotion and she ran towards the room. "Tim!" When she entered the room, she looked around to see Tim sitting in his favorite chair. Broken glass was all over the place. She'd ran to his side, as tears fell from their eyes. She wrapped her arms around him.

"Baby, everything will be alright." She kissed his lips then straddled him. The intensity of their kiss picked up. He lifted her shirt while she helped him remove her pants. Being that he was only wearing boxers, he picked her up and carried her to the bed. For the next two hours they made love to one another.

Niecy cell phone rang while she and Tim held one another. She didn't want to answer it but she did. "Hello."

"Niecy what's up? Trina voice blared through the other end.

"Ain't shit, sitting here with my boo." she shot back.

"Oh." she shot back sounding shocked. "I don't want nothing just checking in on you, tell my brother I said hello."

"Hold on for a second," Niecy said as she passed Tim the phone.

"Hello." Tim said.

"Hey T" she said happy to hear him in good spirits. "I see you and Niecy are back to being a happy couple."

"Yea...yea... where your crazy ass husband at? I been meaning to call him, I just been trying to figure everything out feel me."

"He had to meet with his attorney. I'll tell him to holla at you."

"Alright do that for me."

"Tell Niecy to call me later."

"Gotcha" they ended the call.

Meanwhile in the fifth district police station small interrogation room, with Detective Johnson and Detective Durham, The smell of cigarettes mixed with cheap aftershave was killing Rome sense of smell.

"Jones you think this shit a game?" Detective Durham raised his voice while his partner remained quiet, overlooking a manila envelope of photographs. She looked at Rome shaking her head in disgust. She never imagined him being so weak, so fragile such a bitch. Rome threw both his hands up.

"He's not doing nothing!"

"Bullshit!" Detective Johnson slammed the photos of him, Tim, Tec and Sherrill at his party.

"Look here Jones you can play games with Durham but I'm not the one. I'll have you bail revoked, and make it my personal business to make sure Gamble gets a copy of this statement you made. "Detective Johnson shouted holding up the stacks of papers in her hand, and you and I both know how he'll react if he found out your rat ass was only out to help us arrest him. You're the worst type of man there is, you're the scum of the earth."

She threw the cup of coffee on his face and shirt, I hate rats!"

Rome sat there speechless, her words pierced his soul. He knew he would never be the same again. He sold his soul for some fake ass freedom. What part of the game is that.

Coffee ran down his face and dripped to his already stained shirt. Inside his street instinct wanted to snap her neck, but he knew she was right. He was a rat... Frank Lucas, Rayful Edmonds, Alpo, Sammy the Bull.

"Wait...wait... back off" Detective Durham played the good cop. "He doing his best."

"Fuck that I'll put a copy of this on every drug dealer Facebook page in the city! Fuck with me if you want!" Spit flew from her mouth as she grilled him.

She threw another set of photos before him. When Rome examined the photos he saw Tim and Trina hugged up engaged in a serious conversation. There were at least 15 photos.

"As soon as you got locked up, she ran right to him." She played with Rome mind, she seized the moment and took full advantage of it. He was furious.

"What you think is gonna happen when you're doing twenty years? She'll be in that dick before you know it, maybe she'll name the baby after you." She laughed.

"Ease up, you're going too far, give us a minute please." Detective Durham told his partner.

Rome sat there speechless, coffee soaked shirt, with tears welling in his eyes. He was hurt; the thought of Trina making love to Tim stained his mind. Would they cross me like this? He questioned himself.

Detective Durham knelt beside Rome chair.

"Don't mind her, she a woman, probably on her rag. Listen son, do what we ask of you and all this will be over. You got my word." Durham played his role to the fullest. He noticed Rome eyes were glued to the pictures of Trina and Tim. She's his weakness.

Looking at the two way mirror knowing his partner was listening and watching, he went a bit deeper. "If you love her, then protect her from him. Do the right thing here son."

He stood to his feet, then exited the room. Detective Johnson was in deep thought. "Look at this weak, rat ass nigger, just to think a few years back when she was ripping and running through the Barry farms projects she has a crush on him. Now look, he's a shell of a man. She cracked a smile knowing she'd broken him.

"We got him partner, good job."

They both gave each other a high five.

"Let's get something to eat Detective Johnson said feeling like she was that bitch.

After a thirty minute drive around the city, Rome finally decided to go home. He felt fucked up even had thoughts about driving his car into the river! But his new sense of justification pulled him from doing such a thing. The mere fact that he knew Trina was having an affair was all he needed. Seeing her on Tim's arms replayed over and over in his mind. Tim was going down! Rome entered the bathroom and stared at his reflection. "Slim this nigga want your bitch, get that nigga out the way and save your woman, if you love her, than do what you got to do. He spoke to himself.

It's crazy how right before a nigga get on the stand and help police bring down families. They always justify it with using a bitch, their kids or the infamous they offer a life sentence. A how gonna be a hoe, a nigga gonna be a nigga! No matter what the fuck you think. When he finally exited the bathroom with bloodshot eyes and bags forming from lack of not being able to sleep Trina was watching his every move, like a shark in water she smelled blood, she knew something wasn't right.

"Is everything okay?" she asked, her womanly instincts kicked in, if she knew anybody she knew Rome. She kissed him on the lips and waited for a response. He took a deep breath before he turned to face her. "Baby, I need to tell you something." The look on his face was one she never seen before.

"What's the matter baby?" she held his hand tight, letting him know he could tell her anything.

A single tear dropped from his left eye.

"Trina I fucked up." he spoke just above a whisper and more tears developed in his eyes.

"Baby, what happened?" Trina didn't know what he was going to say, seeing her man so broken was killing her. Rome was always so calm and collective, but strong and supportive. Rome didn't bother to wipe the tears. In his mind he deserved it. Closing his eyes and taking a deep

212

breath. The mere introspective of being labeled a rat was something he couldn't bare.

"Do you remember the morning I left and told you I was going to my lawyer office?" he stared into her eyes then looked away as he continued, "well after I met him we went to the prosecutor's office" he said dropping his head into both his hands feeling like a piece of shit.

And Trina fussed not feeling where she assumed this conversation was going.

"Th...they... threatening to send me back to jail if I didn't snitch on Tim." he stuttered.

"Rome baby tell me you told them to kiss your ass."

He stood to his feet. "I'm not going back to jail."

"Hold the fuck up!" she stood also eye to eye with him.

"Rome I know you didn't agree to set your friend up."

Rome entire facial expression changed.

"Friend!" he shouted to the top of his lungs. "Bitch they showed me the pictures of y'all hugged the fuck up while I was locked up!" he said trying to justify his actions.

Trina couldn't believe what she was hearing. Not only did the only man she'd ever loved beside her dad just admit that he was snitch, he also accused her of cheating with Tim, someone she loved like a brother.

She shook her head, "How could you?"... "You rat mu fucker!"

Before she could finish her sentence, he smacked the spit out her mouth, knocking her to the floor. Taking all his frustrations out on her. He ran over to her and picked her up by her collar and snatched her again. Bow!... he cocked his arm back again. "You disrespectful bitch!" he shouted as he continued to assault her.

"Rome stop it!" she cried as she curled up in a fetal position. Her lips were swollen and her nose was bleeding. As the tears streamed down her face, her mind went into overdrive. At that moment she loved and hated Rome. Rome managed to snap out of his deranged state. Trina I'm sorry please forgive me." he spoke in an apologetic tone trying to console her.

She pulled away from his embrace, snatching her body completely from his grip. "Nigga! Get the fuck away from me! You fucking coward!" she yelled trying her best to get as far away from him as possible.

Tim and Niecy sat on their couch watching Love and Hip Hop on their 72 inch flat screen. Tim had the entire day mapped out. A few movies, an old episode of the Wire, and hot sex until they passed out. His cell phone rang from the coffee table. He checked the caller id seeing it was Trina he smiled as he answered.

"Hey sis."

"Tim...Tim." she blew her nose as she spoke. "I need to see you." she managed to say between cries. "Meet me at the Outback in Largo Town Center please." she spoke just above a whisper.

Instantly he grew upset, "What's wrong Trina?"

"I can't explain this over the phone, just come now please."

"Say no more, I'm on my way."

He hung up the phone then started looking for his shoes. Niecy grew worried for the expression on his face. "Baby is everything alright?"

"I got to go holla at Trina, something is wrong."

Tim drove like a Nascar driver, making record time to Largo Town Center. He found a parking spot so he could watch the entrances and exits, he waited for Trina to arrive. "I wonder what the hell could have went down." he thought as the sound of Raheem Devaughn's Bulletproof filled the air coming out his Bose speakers.

When Trina hung up the phone she spun on her heels only to see Rome standing there. "So you going to meet that nigga! I slap you up and down and you go running to that nigga bitch!" He swung and connected a right hook to her jaw sending her crashing to the floor.

"Ahhh!" she screamed as she went into survival mode, trying her best to defend herself. Rome was all over her punching and kicking her helpless 130 lbs. frame. She managed to kick him square in the balls and brought him to his knees. He cringed in pain. "All shit!"

Seeing an opportunity to get away, she took off toward the living room. It was there she found his glock 45 on the coffee table. Quickly she picked it up, then made her way to their bedroom, she locked the door and cried as she heard Rome calling her.

"Where you at bitch? I'm gonna kill you and that nigga! You hear me you dead bitch!" he tried to open the door but it was locked, he banged and kicked it while threatening to kill her.

"Rome please stop it!" she cried, but her plea fell upon deaf ears as Rome continued to kick the door.

With the weapon in hand she stared at the door, shaking and trembling praying he would leave. Instead he walked to the other end of the hallway so he could ram the door off the hinges.

I'm gonna kill you bitch!"

He ran full speed then dipped his shoulders, knocking it off its grove, shock and fear mixed with adrenaline caused Trina to squeeze the trigger. Not even knowing if the gun was cocked nor loaded, she felt she had no choice. Not knowing that minutes before, Rome was going to take his own life. BOC....BOC....BOC....BOC....BOC....! After the door came crashing off the hinges, then the gunshots. Everything became silent. Trina's vision was blurry and for a mere three minutes, she had no idea what had just taken place. She stood to her feet staring at Rome laying on the floor. Three quarters size holes were in his chest and the once beautiful Persian rug was now filled with crimson. Rome body was motionless, he wasn't breathing. He was dead. Trina hands went to her face as she processed what had just took place. The tears she was looking for would not allow themselves to fall. The echo of her father voice stained her ears.

"A man who takes his own weight." replayed in her head she could not mirror with the gun still in her hand, She took off to her car leaving Rome in a puddle of blood.

Tim grew impatient as a few minutes turned into an hour. He became frustrated, calling Trina cellphone, he finally heard the engine of her car parked next to his. He looked over and the expression on her face alarmed him that something was wrong. He exited the car, then hopped in her passenger side of her 650 BMW. He first took a notice to her swollen eyes, and dry blood stained cheeks. He looked down and seen the blood all over her blouse, and pants. But what stood out to him the most was how her hands were shaking. The silence was tense, the look on her face was distraught, he gave her space and allowed her time.

"Tim..." she said in a whisper. "Rome wasn't right!"

"What you mean?" he asked assuming Rome must've beat her.

"Tim, I..I..." she tried to get the words out, but she was having a hard time.

He placed his hand in hers, letting her know that everything would be alright. Feeling that assurance, she was able to speak. "Tim I just killed Rome."

"What the!" he was about to explode till she cut him off. Still staring straight ahead. "Rome was a rat!" she allowed her words to sink in too him.

"He cooperated against you." she finally turned to face him.

I'll k...kill him..., I shot, shot him. A single tear rolled down her face.

She then reached towards the middle console, grabbing her YSL clutch bag.

Tim tried to process what he just heard, Rome ratted him out. He thought while staring at Trina. "Bitch ass nigga crossed me like that."

"Trina what happened?"

She wiped her eyes, then told him everything from start to finish, sparing no details. All he could do was shake his head as Trina spoke. Trina reached in her purse then pulled out the murder weapon, a Glock 45, then passed it to Tim.

"I'll take care of this Trina, here take this, he reached into his pocket pulling out a wad of bills, then passed it to her.

"Trina go to the hotel, get cleaned up and call me when you finish, if anybody ask, after Rome came home you went shopping and left him alone."

"How can I explain my face? If I get a room I'll look guilty."

Tim had to agree with her logic. "Okay... take this key, there's a hide away spot in the Carter, change your clothes and call me."

He took the key off the ring. "Apartment 612, okay?"

She took the key then held his hand then reached out to hug him, as they held their embrace she did that unthinkable. Thinking he was letting go, she slipped her tongue in his mouth, crazy thing about it was instead of pushing her away he welcomed it. Now Tim was a stand up nigga, and never crossed anybody who didn't deserve it. But his natural attraction to her, got the best of him. She let go and they stared at one another. With nothing else said, he tucked the murder weapon under his shirt and exited the car.

"Fuck...Fuck...Fuck...!" Tim shouted as he banged on the steering wheel as he drove home. Tears ran down his face the thought of Rome selling his soul to the pigs, the federal government was enough to make him throw up. Instantly he picked up the phone to call Niecy. "Bey, get dressed! I'll be there in a minute." He hung up. "Is my phone tapped? How much did he tell these fucking feds" he questioned himself as he drove. "I gotta get rid of this pistol." He was nearing his exit to his home, he was minutes away.

When Tim entered the home, Niecy too notice of the look on his face. "Baby, what's wrong?"

"Let's go now!"

He exited back out he house, Niecy followed suit, she secured the door then jumped in the car.

"Mr. Jones!...Mr. Jones!" Agent Jenkins yelled from the outside of Rome home. He was growing impatient he had a fourteen hour ride ahead of him and was eager to get on the road. Rome witness protection has been approved to a sweet location in Leavenworth, Kansas, until Tim's trial was over.

With Tim in custody, and Rome testimony, Tim was sure to receive the minimum of a life sentence for murder, weapon charges and conspiracy to possess and distribute 500 grams of cocaine. Seeing the front door was ajar, agent Jenkins made his way inside the home. Looking around seeing the home was in disarray, he pulled his weapon and canvassed the area, checking the bathroom then the kitchen, a spec of blood caught his attention. Following the trail of blood, he saw Rome laid in a puddle of blood. "I need backup.... I repeat I need backup now!"

When Niecy entered the car she realized she left her keys in the door.

"Hold on boo, I left my keys in the door."

She quickly got out the car to retrieve her keys from the front door. As she grabbed them, sounds of footsteps and a car slamming on brakes caught her attention. She looked over, the sight of automatic weapons and figures dressed in black with DEA and ATF written across their front, scared her to death.

"T-I-M!" she screamed to the top of her lungs. By then it was too late they had Tim's car surrounded.

"Get the fuck out the car! Show me them fucking hands now!" one of the officers yelled.

Tim looked around, and then processed the situation at hand.

"Shit!" He thought about smashing the gas and going for it, but quickly he dismissed the thought.

"BABY!" Niecy yelled as he was slammed to the car.

Tim was snatched out the car, he and Niecy stood face to face over the hood. "You better not cry! You better not shed one motherfucking tear!" Tim managed to say while they roughed him up.

"Is there a problem officers?" There must be some mistake." Tim smiled knowing his lawyer would tear the government a new ass hole.

"Do you have a warrant?"

One of the officers pulled the Glock 45 from under the seat, along with his personal 9 millimeter from the glovebox. The smile instantly disappeared.

Detective Tonya Johnson walked over to Niecy, and put her hand on her shoulders attempting to play the good cop, and use the female role to press her vulnerability.

"Hey, I'm Detective Johnson. What's your name?" she said while giving her a once over admiring her heel game.

Niecy ignored her. Detective Johnson instantly became upset by her rudeness.

"Oh you can't talk hun?" she closed the distance between the two of them.

"I'll bet you'll talk when I take your ass down to the station." Niecy just stared at her, and didn't say a word.

"Look, maybe we got off on the wrong foot. Right now I can charge you with accessory to murder and a lot of other things."

Niecy rolled her eyes and laughed.

"Did I say something funny, I'll see if you find something funny when you standing in front of the judge.. "Detective Johnson lost her cool.

"Get them the fuck outta here!"

Tim and Niecy were placed in separate squad cars. The tinted out ford explorer gave him an eerie feeling. This is the same tinted explorer he'd seen several times. Both Tim and Niecy watched as twenty plus police officers rushed inside their home. Tim shook his head as the car pulled off. On the ride to the homicide office, Detective Durham called Detective Stone to inform him that he had Tim in custody. Tim listened to the phone conversation, the simple fact that the police showed so much joy in his demise, ran a chill through his body.

"Hope my lawyer can handle this bullshit." He thought as he watched the scenery. When they finally pulled up to the station, he watched the officers take Niecy to the elevator. His heart broke as he looked on. After she was taken away, he was removed from the squad car, holding his head high, he was lead to the same elevator they put Niecy on.

Trina has just finished showering in the vacant apartment in the Carter. Although the building was drug infested, and full of crackheads, hookers and pimps. This particular apartment was cozy. After drying off and touching up her makeup to cover her wounds, she slipped on a pair of french connection jeans and matching t-shirt. She plopped down on the couch and flipped on the television to catch the news.

"I can't believe I kissed Tim" she mumbled to herself.

The thought of what transpired between them, for some reason, between all the madness around her somehow her pussy got wet. Her hand made its way to her wetness, when the face of a man appeared on the screen. He was in front of her house. And there were cops everywhere. She aimed the remote at the TV to turn up the volume.

This is Lisa Henry, coming to you for the Channel Five News. I stand here in Accokeek, MD where the arrest of Mr. Tim Gamble had just taken place. The local authorities along with ATF and DEA surrounded the house where he was taken into custody. He's being charged with the murder of Darrell and Donald Miller. It's speculation of retaliation for the murder of Tim's brother, the deceased Tony Gamble. Also in connection for a murder in Atlanta, Georgia, and a murder at the Zanzibar nightclub in Southwest DC....

Wait a minute.... What was that Jim? Wait, this just in... The weapon found in Mr. Gamble's vehicle matched the murder weapon that killed Mr. Rome Jones. It's said that Mr. Jones was a confidential informant, who was about to be taken to WITSEC, a witness protection program setup by the federal government. Mr. Gamble is responsible for 30% of the cocaine trade in the DC area. He is also being charged with conspiracy to distribute 100 kilos of cocaine. It's safe to say the citizens of the DMV are happy thig mad man is off the streets. This is Lisa Henry, back to you Jim.

Trina breath was lost, she wasn't breathing and began sweating. "OH MY GOD!" she shouted. NO...NO...NO...!

From afar she heard commotion barely being able to stand; she looked out the window to see the Carter was surrounded with police officers.

Tim sat in an interrogation room staring at the two way mirrors, knowing officer were behind the glass. "What the fuck did Rome tell these peoples?" he questioned his own thoughts.

Detective Durham entered the room with his partner Detective Johnson right behind him. She sat in front of Tim while Durham stood. Detective Johnson cleared her throat. "Umm...Umm... I know you're what we consider ole school, so we you to help your self is out the question. I want you to know this is a State and Federal charge, you'll be lucky to get the death penalty. Your lawyer will be here shortly. She slid a manila envelope across the table. "This is what your best friend Mr. Jones had to say."

She stood then looked at her partner and exited the room with Durham in tow. Tim sat silent as he opened the envelope. A 237 page statement. Rome spilled his guts about the Miller brother murders, Poes murder at the Club U. Refusing to drop a tear, Tim stood his ground and shook his head. "Hot mufucker." he thought knowing that life as he know it was over.

Chapter 12

Detective Tonya Johnson sat behind her desk, knowing she had nothing on Niecy. Just the pure fact she could, she ran Niecy down to the station, being ornery she justified her action by the way Niecy acted when she was being questioned. Detective Durham went along with his partner, even though he was tired of seeing so many women getting arrested behind some shit there man was involved in.

Niecy walked out the fifth district police station an hour later, after being released she flagged down a cab, then hopped in the back seat. After giving the driver the directions she looked out the window back toward the station happy to get as far away from there. The cab driver looked thru his rear view mirror and could see the sadness, plastered on Niecy face. Knowing that her other half was still being detained was tearing her little heart in pieces...... Thirty minutes later the cab pulled in front of Niecy and Tim home. Niecy peeped out the window praying that none of her neighbors were out. After paying her fare, she hopped out the cab then walked into the place she called home. Knowing that living in that big ole house without her man would never be the same, she looked around at all the things that they had accumulated over the years, they were all meaningless, the only thing that meant anything to her at that moment was to get her man home. She grabbed the house phone off the stand, then dialed Tim lawyer Jennifer Wicks.

"Law office of Jennifer Wicks!"

"May I speak to Mrs. Wicks?"

Who's calling?"
Denice White... Tim Gamble's wife.

"Hold on for a minute please!"

"Jennifer!"

"Hello Mrs. Wicks, have you heard anything?

"Well I just left the station, and Tim is scheduled to appear in front of a judge for a bond hearing. Tim should arrive in the district court before I get there but once I get there I should know a little more after I speak with him and the prosecutor.

"Alright Mrs. Wicks I'll see you tomorrow.

Sherrill laid across her bed exhausted from the 10 miles she had run thru Haines Pointe park with only taking a shower and then some good rest on her mind when her cell began ringing. She grabbed her cell of the night stand then looked at the caller ID before answering.

"Hey Lee!"

"Sherrill did you see the news?"

"Naw what happen?"

"Your friend Tim is on all the news channels for killing his friend Rome." Sherrill grabbed the remote and surf thru every news channel till she found Tim being taken into a police station, handcuffed with two police officers.

"Damn!" Sherrill said not believing her eyes. "Lee this shit is crazy, they were close like brothers at least that's what Tim told me.

"Lee I call you back!"

"Okay girl but you alright?"

"Yea I'm good!"

"Alright girl hit me later!"

Sherrill hung up the phone then set up in her bed with her legs bent up, with both fist balled up against her face. "Damn boo" was all she could say as she digested the fact that Tim was being charged with murdering his friend. A smile crossed her face as she reminisced back to the night when they first met. In her eyes Tim was a gentleman, thug, smooth lover with much swagger, but what she liked most was the way he demanded respect, she hopped out the bed and stripped naked then walked in her bathroom to take a shower.

Tim was sitting at the back of the van that transported inmates from the police station to the court building, smelling like death, he was happy to finally get some fresh air after sleeping in a cage full of alcoholics and addicts that smell like they haven't bathed in months. The whole ride the only thing on his mind was the reason he was in the predicament he was in, his love for the person that he would have took a bullet to the head for.

"Damn I know how the mob felt after finding out that hot ass Sammy the Bull turned star witness against them." He thought to himself knowing the information Rome gave on him, he knew he could receive a life sentence. The fact that Rome was dead brought a smile to his face, hopes of returning back to society, then all sort of thoughts began running thru his head. Did Trina set me up to take the murder rap, was she part of it or was it a coincidence? Damn she never tried to kiss me that way that was unusual of her he said to himself.

Niecy walked in the courtroom looking radiant as ever, feeling tears rolling down her cheeks, then

Tim voice was in her head, you better not shed a fucking tear.

She wiped them away with the back of hand and proceeded to walk in the courtroom like a soldier ready to be deployed she went straight to the front row then sat next to Tim mother Pat. The courtroom was packed with news reporters from all new channels, to some of Tim's friends and foes, there was even a few of the hood gossip reporters ready to add and take something out to spread a juicy story. After the prosecutor slandered Tim's character, Tim's lawyer Jennifer Wicks pleaded and campaigned for a bond for Tim, but the judge denied bond.

Niecy looked over at Tim with a shocked expression on her face. In Tim's mind her knew with the police finding the gun on him with his prints on it that killed Rome and with all the information Rome gave against him even if he had O.J. Simpson's old lawyer Johnny Cochran he wouldn't have been able to pull off him getting a bond. Niecy was still staring at him with a million questions in her eyes, Tim whispered in his hired mouthpiece Jennifer Wicks ear before the marshals led him back into the back of the courtroom. Niecy looked around thru the courtroom till she locked eyes with Detective Tonya Johnson with a smile on her face, looking like she had just hit the Powerball. Niecy rolled her eyes then stood up and followed Pat out the courtroom.

"You see that bitch Durham?" Detective Johnson said to her partner.

"Yea I do Johnson." He said wondering why she was harboring bad feelings towards Niecy.

Curly sat in his office in the back of Club Stadium in his study desk, arms folded staring at a picture of Tim the night of Rome's party. "Damn so I would have protected you from this bullshit, I should have made it my business to get you out the game." He thought to himself eyes trained on the picture. A knock on the door brought him back from his thoughts.

Knock...Knock...Knock!

"Come in!" Curly called towards the door.

The door opened and Curly best friend and partner Big Cotten walked in with his big frame. He stood 6'6" 240 solid. "What's good slim?" Cotten said noticing his best friend has a disturbed look on his face. Cotten looked over following Curly eyes staring at the picture of Tim. "Curly have you spoken to Pat?" Cotten said changing the subject.

"Naw not yet."

"Curly I know that it's fucked up that he got locked up before you had a chance to let him know you was his father. But you gotta keep your head up like the champion you is. And I got on top everything."

Three Weeks Later

Trina looked over at the Potomac River with teary eyes, ever since Rome's death she debated what she was going do next. Ever since they set eyes on each other immediately they became an item. Before the money, the cars, and big house, they were head over heels for one another. Even as a teenager Rome was always a standup guy, with good morals and principles. He had a full time job, a paper route and sold hot dogs at the Redskins stadium, Trina was beautiful and very intelligent, it only took five months in their relationship for the couple to know that it was time to get married.

They went to the courthouse and filled out the required papers to unite them as one. The next day they were officially Mr. and Mrs. Jones. Even though Rome flirted with other women time to time he never cheated. In Rome's eyes Trina was everything that he wanted and the feelings was mutual as far as Trina was concerned but at that particular moment she hated him more than the man that killed her parents and raped her when she was only ten years old.

"You rat motherfucker. How could your bitch ass snitch, and on a mu'fucker that would have done anything that a friend could do for you and more. She opened the box filled with Rome ashes then tossed it in the river, she turned around and walked away as if he never meant a thing to her.

Once Tim arrived at DC Jail he and over 150 inmates were escorted off three different buses, shackled and handcuffed, DC Jail is one of the most dangerous jails in America. Which houses every kind of inmate's stabbings and rape. If you wasn't prepared to take a life, then check the fuck in solitary confinement, because you might lose your life or even your manhood or both. Tim looked around at a few other inmates, seeing of he noticed someone he might had an old beef with.

Even though he was out of his normal environment, he refused to let a nigger at the ups on him. As he looked over to his left, he noticed a curly head black dude staring him down. The dude nodded his head in a friendly gesture. Tim nodded back then checked his memory bank trying to figure where he knew the dude from. He still couldn't figure out if he knew the dude. The dude whispered in another inmate ear and they walk inside the jail into a holding a cell. As Tim entered the jail he looked around in search of the dude then noticed him and the same dude he was speaking to outside standing in a cell.

Niecy was cruising on the BW Parkway singing along with Ledis from her pioneer speakers headed to the DC jail. Tim was extradited to DC jail to face the murder charge of the Orlean crew. Knowing how the feds worked, she kept her eyes on the road and her rearview mirrors, checking to see if she was being tailed. Tim always told her if someone was following her, it wouldn't be the car right behind her, it would be the car a few cars back. She switched on her blinkers alerting the other cars on the highway that she was about to switch lanes.

After driving a few feet she switched off her blinkers after feeling comfortable that she wasn't being followed. Once she arrived at the jail she was anxious to see her boo, she looked in her mirror checking to make sure her mac lip gloss was perfectly applied on her juicy lips. Then she hopped out of her X5 and looked over at the long line of women and men and children waiting to see their loved one, not caring if the long line was stretched from Maine to Florida she was going to wait and see her man.

"Lee…. I know Moody is happy as shit to get his appeal over turn."

"Yea he is, but soon as he get out I know he going try to beat my ass for not coming to visit him…. I know he got the right to be mad but bitch it is what it is I didn't tell him to get locked the fuck up.

Sherrill just sat there listening, not agreeing or disagreeing, even though she knew that Lee carried Moody fucked up while he was locked up. Lee was her best friend and however he felt she and Lee would deal with it then, him putting his hand on Lee was not an option. Sherrill looked over and noticed someone that she never imagined to see walking in the visitor room looking around trying to find his visitor looking handsome as ever he took a seat.

"Oh my God," Sherrill said with a smile on her face, her smile was brighter than some jewelry at Jake the Jewelers. "Lee I'll be right back!" She said as she hopped out her seat and walked over to an empty seat in front of none other than Tim. A smile creased his face seeing Sherrill on the other side of the glass. He grabbed the phone then motioned for her to pick up the phone.

"Hey Shawty" he spoke with much swag.

"Hey you!" She replied with a smile on her face like a bride about to get married at the altar. "Tim how you holding up?"

"I'm good!"

"That's good to hear. "Boy after I saw you on the news I became worried about you."

Tim didn't respond, instead his eyes grew larger than a golf ball, after seeing the on Niecy's face walking in his direction. He knew he was going to have a hard time explaining to Niecy, Sherrill being there was just a coincidence.

"Hello!" Niecy spoke to Sherrill with a devilish smirk on her face not caring if she picked up on it.

"Alright Tim you take care of yourself." Sherrill said before walking off.

"O yea mu'fucka!" Niecy spat with spit flying out her mouth.

He knew Sherrill sitting there wouldn't go right with Niecy but her refuse to allow her to make a scene in front of all the people in the crowded visiting hall, he gave her a look that said now wasn't the time then he motion for her to pick up the phone.

"Hey baby!" Tim said.

"Don't hey baby me."

Instead of grilling him about Sherrill, Lord God she wanted to, she refrain herself due to his situation.

"What's up cheater?"

"Go ahead with that bullshit! Have you heard from Trina?"

"Naw every time I called her phone went to voicemail."

"Oh yea!" he said looking out the corner of his eye.

"So you going to disrespect me by looking at that bitch…. You know what, fuck you Tim I'm out, you can keep looking at that bitch, as a matter fact, tell that bitch she can have your sorry disrespectful ass, and also tell her to do that time with you they going give your bitch ass.

She slammed the phone on the receiver making sure Sherrill and everybody else in there could have heard her. She hopped out her seat and strutted toward the elevator with no intention of ever coming back. This nigga got me fucked up, he musta lost his fucking mind to have that bitch sitting all in his face knowing damn well I was on my way. His ass locked up and he still got enough balls to disrespect me. She got inside her X5 then headed to the one person that knew Tim better than he knew himself.

Niecy pulled up in front of Tim mother house and hopped out her truck she marched into the house after using the key mom Pat gave her.

"Hey mom!" Niecy spoke.

Pat was sitting in the day room watching TV then looked up and smiled.

"Hey baby!" Pat said giving her a hug and kiss on the cheek. What brings you over so early I thought you was going to see Tim?

"I just left his stupid ass…. Now I need someone to talk too.

"What he done now?"

"Mom you won't believe his stupid ass had some chick in the visiting room, cheesing all in his face when I walked in." Even though Tim was her child, she would never justify his actions, she would always say right is right and wrong is wrong. She knew Niecy loved him just as much as Tim loved her.

"Niecy baby I'm not telling you not to be upset, but right now he going thru a lot and is going to need you!"

Niecy shook her head in agreement. "Yea I know and I'm mad as hell, but I love his stupid ass."

Pat smiled wrapping her arms around her. That boy gets that shit from his father! Pat said with a disturbed look on her face.

"You alright?" Niecy asked seeing her looking as if she was having a moment.

"Yea baby…. I'm good."

Pat was usually a strong woman, that moment she looked weaker than a 100lb crackhead trying to lift 900lb of weights.

"You love him?"

"Yes, I loved him like I never loved no other man."

Pat was wearing a smile brighter than the sky on a sunny day. She told Niecy how she met him, and how she got pregnant with Tim and Tony, and how she never told him., instead she called him, then told him she never wanted to see him again. He kept calling and coming around, until she changed her number and moved across town. When she finally decided to tell him she found out from a mutual friend that he was locked up in the feds. She never told the twins who their father was, she let them think it was the man that help raise the, was their father. The twins never got along with him, especially when they came home seeing her crying from his beating her. The day Tim found out he was murdered in an alley off Maryland Avenue, he didn't shed not one tear. Pat was about to go on until she heard a knock on her door. She walked over then peeped thru the peep hole. After seeing who was on the other end of her door, she opened it.

"Well speak of the devil!" Pat said stirring at Curly.

"O yea... I been called a lot of things but never the devil."

Pat ignored him and turned to Curly best friend. "Hello Cotten!"

"Hey Pat, how you been?" he said sticking his arms out for a friendly hug.

"I'm holding on." Pat said trying her best not to wrap her arms around his big 210 frame.

"Hey... hey the devil can't get a hug?" Curly asked.

Pat looked over at him...AW... no!, Curly this is Tim fiancé Niecy!"

"Hello Niecy it's nice to meet you!" he said politely in a smooth tone.

"It's nice to meet you as well."

Niecy couldn't keep her eyes from him, Tim was a spitting image of him, besides the specks of gray sprinkled in his beard. She knew where Tim got his good taste of fashion from. Curly was wearing a black Heme shirt, slacks and a pair of Heme loafers.

"So Niecy when was the last time you spoke to him?" Curly asked.

"I just left the jail right before I came here!"

"How he holding up?"

"He still Tim!"

Curly mind flashed back to the night of Rome party, smiling to himself, knowing Niecy wasn't the same woman he was with at the club. "That boy got a good taste of women." he thought to himself.

Niecy could hear her cell phone vibrating in her purse indicating she had a call. She quickly retrieved it from her purse, hoping it was her boo so she could apologize for the way she acted in the visiting room. She checked her caller ID before answering.

"Trina hold on for a second!"

She excused herself before she stepped off to the kitchen to take the call.

"Trina where have you been girl, and why haven't you been answering my calls?"

"Niecy I'm sorry I just been going thru so much... can you meet me somewhere?"

Niecy thought about it for a second being the last time she called Tim got locked up.

"Yea meet me at the arboretum in 20 minutes!"

"Alright I'll be there!"

After hanging up from Trina, Niecy came out and said her goodbyes, and promised Pat she would call her later. Pat house was 5 minutes away. Niecy made sure she was there to make sure Trina didn't arrive with some unexpected guest.

Once Niecy arrived she found a parking space a few cars away from the entrance of the Arboretum. The Arboretum was a quiet National park off Bladensburg Road, where mostly tourist visits. They have all different sorts of flowers and trees from around the world. Niecy hopped out her X5, then walked around in search of five-o.

Niecy spotted Trina when she pulled up and dialed her cell.

"Hey girl where you at?" Trina asked.

"I'm right behind you, park and come hop in my truck!"

"Alright!"

Niecy never wanted to believe that Trina would do anything to put her life in danger, but growing up in her hood she saw so many people turn snitch. For their so called freedom, that it was unbelievable. Trina hoped in the truck, she told Niecy everything that happened from Rome snitching to him beating her for calling him a rat, to pulling the trigger that took his life, she even told how she had Rome body cremated, and how she tossed his ashes in the river, the only thing she held back was the accusation Rome made accusing her and Tim of messing around.

Niecy listened carefully, feeling bad for her, in her heart she wanted to tell Trina to go take her charge and free her man. Even if she would have, she knew Tim wouldn't allow it with good morals and principal that he stood for made Niecy made Niecy love him more. Niecy looked over at Trina, "T everything going to be alright, we will work it out, go get in your car and follow me out the house, I know you don't want to go back to your house yet!"

Detective Tonya Johnson and her Partner Durham sat in the warden office with a signed warrant to listen to Tim phone calls. Det. Johnson explained to the warden how she and the US Attorney office was greatly appreciative of him, helping them take down one DC biggest drug dealers of the streets.

Tim walked out his cell he spotted the big dude he had the issue with about the phone, walking towards him, looking like a silverback gorilla.

"I wish this nigga would!" Tim thought to himself not one to run from a fight.

Seeing the way Tim swole up with his fist balled up, the big dude knew he has to calm him down.

"Hold up Slim, I come in peace!" the big dude said in a friendly tone. Tim didn't respond.

"Slim I apologize about earlier, I didn't know you was from northeast!" Tim kept his eyes trained on him like a pitbull, wondering how he knew where he was from. The big dude reached in his pocket and pulled out a folded letter, then passed it to him. Tim unfolded it then began reading it. WHAT'S GOOD BIG SLIM, THIS MOODY THE DUDE THAT HOLLA AT CHU GETTING OFF THE BUS. SHERELL FRIEND, LEE BABYFATHER, ME AND YOUR BROTHER USE TO PLAY BALL TOGETHER. LEE TOLD ME WHAT WENT DOWN WITH SHERELL AND YOUR PEOPLE. I MUST'VE JUST MISSED YOU, BUT IF YOU NEED ANYTHING, AND I MEAN ANYTHING, HOLLA AT MY MAN BOGGA, THE ONE THAT GAVE YOU THIS LETTER. TRY TO COME TO CHURCH SUNDAY SO WE CAN HOOK UP. PEACE....

Tim looked up and noticed the two dudes that was with Biggs earlier, walking up with two bags of commissary.

"This is for you from Moody!" Bigga said passing him the bags. And my bad about the phone.

"Shit don't sweat it, no harm done, but I still need to use that phone!"

"Say no more!" Bigga said with a big goofy grin on his face.

After tossing the commissary in his cell Tim went and grabbed the phone to call Niecy.

All the other inmates was watching him, shocked how he came back and use the phone after Bigga told him not to.

Niecy was almost home when her cell rang, she reached over passenger seat and picked it up. Hello!

"You have a prepaid call from the department of correction from…. Tim, if you would like to accept this call press 5.

"Hello!" Niecy said after pressing 5

"Niecy what's up?"

"What's up with you baby?" she said as if she hadn't showed out the last time she was with him.

"TIM I'M SORRY FOR THE WAY I ACTED OUT.... BOY WHEN I SAW THAT BITCH SMILING ALL IN YOUR FACE, I JUST LOST IT.

"Yea you tripped the fuck out you didn't give me a chance to explain, everything not how it look.

"Yea I know!"

"Niecy you don't have to worry about me cheating on you again... Baby I learned my lesson.

"You better have cause if it happen again, I'm gonna kill your ass, you hear me cheater!"

"Yea...Yea I hear you baby!"

"Tim why you just calling me?"

"That's a long story, but the phone about to cut off, they about to lock us down for the night, so I see you tomorrow. Niecy I need you to stop and get a prepaid phone and I'll tell you what to do with it tomorrow when you come, I lov...." was all she heard before the phone cut off.

Dat was sitting in front of the Carter in his black on black tinted out Aston Martin, with his dick bone cement hard. He took off his Versace sunshades to get a better view at the female sashaying her way in his direction. She stopped in front of his driver side geeking he rolled the window down.

"O...My bad I thought you were someone else!" she said lying out her ass."

"Ma...Ma...Maybe I ca.. Can help you!"

"Naw I'm good," she said staring at his car. This is a nice car!"

Nina was mesmerized off the big chunky diamonds glistening from the Rolex. Dat hopped out the car looking like a rapper about to shoot a rap video. Nina has saw guys bling Dat was bling blowing.

"Hello I'm Nina."

"Yo..you from up north?"

"Yea... New York."

"I..I.. could tell."

Nina had to stop herself from laughing from the way he stuttered. She wasn't going to let that stop her from hooking up with him. If she could deal with Bubble old busted body ass, she had no problem with fucking around with a fly ass stuttering nigger.

"So Nina you live around here?"
"Naw my family runs that barber shop over there!" she said pointing over to Bubble shop.

"Is tha...that right!"

"So Dat what brings you around here?"
"Just came to see if anybody heard from a friend of mine that got arrested out here."

It didn't take a rocket scientist to know he was talking about... Nina was ready to cut into him like a knife in butter. She licked her lips in a seductive way, laying bait, trying to get some kind of reaction from him.

"Well Dat it was nice meeting you!" She began walking away shaking her ass, making sure it jiggled.

"Hol... hold up!"

Nina knew she had him, her ass was fatter than a fifty dollar onion.

"Ta..Ta..Take my number, maybe we cou..could go get something to eat, and get to know each other."

She stopped then turned around. Dat eyes roamed her body from head to toe. Nina could see the bulge in his pants and she wanted it badly, she felt a tingle between her thighs, then a warm wetness, she was having an orgasm just staring at his print. She had thoughts of his dick in her pussy. "Yea let's do that."

Dat flipped open his cell then they exchanged numbers. Dat programmed Nina number in his cell. She did the same.

"Well Dat, I'll give you a call."

"Cool!"
Nina strutted off while Dat kept his eyes glued on her ass.

Niecy rolled over form out a deep sleep, after being awakened from the vibration of her cell phone. She reached her arms out toward her night stand, almost knocking her cell to the floor. She grabbed her cell and hit the talk button. She had a feeling it was Tim calling and she was going to make sure she spoke to him. The operator was on the other end.

"You have a prepaid call from the Department of Corrections, if you would like to speak..."

Niecy didn't let the recording continue.

"Hey baby!" she said smiling thru the phone.

"What's up boo?" Tim replied.

"Tim I love you!"

He chuckled, "I love you too."

"Baby you have to come home." she said sounding like a whining child.

"You ain't got too tell me!"
"Tim you won't believe who stayed over last night."

"Who!"

"Trina"

"O yea where she at?"

"She in the guest room."

"Niecy put her on the phone."
"Alright...hold on for a second.

She hopped out the bed, then threw her robe on and walked to the guest room. She tapped on the door then walked in. Trina was cuddled up under a comforter and some warm sheets. Trina looked up.

"Trina, Tim on the phone he want to speak with you."

Niecy passed her the cell, Trina was happy and sad at the same time, knowing she played a part of him being in his predicament, giving him the gun that killed her hot ass husband. She began to cry.

"Trina don't cry!" Tim said.

"Tim I'm sorry. I swear I...

He cut her off. "Trina...everything going to be alright, but you have to watch how you talk on these phones, you know these people record these phone calls, then they change your words around and use them against you."

"I miss you brother!"
"I miss you too sis, we are family and no matter what we gotta stick together."

"Trina I'm going to need you to go see my lawyer with Niecy."

"Okay Tim."

"I love you sis, make sure you come with Niecy to see me tomorrow"

"I will!"

"Put Niecy on the phone."

No matter what Rome did, it had nothing to do with Trina, in his eyes Trina would always be family. It's rare these days that a woman would go against their man, when finding out he's a rat. Six out of ten would've went along with his hot ass, and would've packed up and moved across the country in some witness protection program.

Trina passed the phone to Niecy, then Tim explained to her how important it was for her to make sure she kept Trina strong, and to set up a meeting with Trina and his lawyer Jennifer Wicks.

"Tim when I walk in that visiting room and you have another bitch in your face, I swear to God somebody going to get fucked up and it ain't gonna be me!"

He laughed, but he knew she was dead serious. "Go head with that bullshit!"

"O nigga you think it's a game! Go ahead with that bullshit!"

"Yea.. Yea I hear you!"

After listening to Tim's phone recording, Detective Johnson couldn't believe what she just heard. She looked over at her partner Durham with venom in her eyes. "Durham… can you believe this shit, unfucking believable!" she stated.

"Yea Johnson, they definitely was fucking, that's the reason Gamble probably killed Jones."

"No shit Sherlock!'

Tim walked out his cell feeling a little more comfortable knowing that Moody and his crew had his back, if he needed them. Being the dud he was, he trusted no one with his life. If shit would have pop off he wanted to be prepared not knowing what nobody else would have done he knew for sure what he would do, even if it took him catching a body. He walked up on Bigga, who was playing dominoes.

"What's up Bigga?"

"Ain't shit my nigga!" Bigga said slamming down the dominoes. "Dominoes nigga!" he said to the guy he was playing. "Tim you play this shit?"
"Naw slim, chess my thing, but um I need to holla at you for a minute."

Bigga stood up and told the dude he'd be back. He and Tim walked off toward the other end of the unit away from all the other inmates. Tim was never the one to beat around the bush.

"Bigga I need a banger!"

"What up slim, you got beef?"

"Naw I'm good I just like to be ready, I'm not with all that talking shit, if I got beef, I 'ma deal with it as I see fit, you feel me."

Bigga shook his head in agreement, "Yea I got you, meet me in your cell in 20 minutes."

"Bet!" Tim said sticking his fist out to give him a pound.

Tim was sitting in his cell and like Bigga said he was there for him. Bigga knocked on Tim cell door, Tim waved him in. Bigga peeped around then creeped in the cell.

"Here go slim!" Bigga said passing Tim a nine inch bark street knife, the kind you would find at an Army Surplus store.

"That's what I'm talking about... What I owe you?"

"You good."

"That's what up!" Bigga I appreciate this, and I'm definitely going to return the favor.

Dat pulled in Jasper parking lot with his lil homie Vedo who had just came home from the feds. Vedo was scoping out all the different cars and trucks in the parking lot. While locked up Vedo heard how Jaspers be jumping off, seeing the Bentley, Audi R8, Ferrari, reassured him about what he had heard. While locked up he heard Dat was doing it big. When Dat picked him up in his Aston Martin he knew it for himself. Dat was getting money but he would spend it just as fast as he made it, he was a fool, but he wasn't a damn fool. He knew with Tim being locked up, if he didn't hurry and find a new connect he would soon go broke especially the way he spend money.

John Wall and a few other Washington Wizards were walking in with a couple of females that look like they were models. RG3 and a big guy around 6'8" 280lbs walked in. Dat looked over at Vedo. "V!" Dat said seeing the way Vedo was looking star struck.

"V...I might don't have tha..that NFL, or N-B-Aaa money. But nig- nigga I hold my own. He reached on his hip and pulled out a Glock 40 with an extended clip then placed it in his arm rest. Looking over at Vedo making sure he saw he was packing. Vedo knew Dat wasn't with no gun play, he knew Dat was known for paying someone to put in work. Before Vedo got locked up he was well known for busting his guns. As soon as they walked in the restaurant all they could see was nothing but female ass. Dat was enjoying the scenery, He waved a waitress over and asked to be seated close by the front door. Being the hot boy he was, he wanted to make sure he was seen by any and everybody that came thru. Sherrill and Lee were sitting at a table drinking and enjoying themselves. Lee hopped up when the DJ started playing Wale new song Bad Girl, she started dancing like a video vixen. She was getting her groove on, not caring who was watching. She was rubbing her hands around her breasts, then spun around shaking her ass like a salt shaker. Sherrill laughed to herself, thinking you can take a freak out but you can't take the freak out a freak. Sherrill looked over to her right and noticed a short Mexican was staring at her, he smiled then whispered into the ear of one of the two big Mexicans that was standing next to him. Then started walking over, the two Mexicans was following close behind him until he waved them off, then he continued to walk over.

"Hola como estas?" he said meaning how are you.

"Bueno tu!" she responded in her best Spanish. Meaning good and you.

"Bien!" he answered. Meaning good

He rubbed his cheeks and smiled. "Tu ablas! (you speak Spanish)

She shook her head "Si!" (yes)

He looked over at Lee on the dance floor dancing like she was in a strip club, then he looked back at Sherrill then stuck his hands out "Guard!"

She took his hand. "Hello Guardo..... I'm Sherrill!" she said and released his hands. His hands was freshly manicured they were softer than cotton. She looked him up and down. "If I'm not mistaken I thought Guardo meant fat boy!

"Well let's just say I use to carry some extra weight when I was a lil younger, and the name just stuck with me!" he said with a sexy smile.

Guardo was small in size around 5'3" 130 lbs. caramel brown with jet black hair with a set of pearly whites. He was wearing a Hugo boss suit that had him looking sharper than a butcher knife.

"Well Sherrill after seeing your pretty face, I had to come and speak before God realized that one of his angels was missing!"

"Damn he good!" she thought to herself, even though she knew it was a line.

"I know you say that to all the ladies!"

He looked her in her eyes looking sincere. "No you are the first. Sherrill would you take my number and give me a call!" he said on his Charlie last name Wilson shit.

"Sure I'll take your number!"

He reached in his wallet and pulled out a card, then passed it to her, she wrote down the number on a napkin and handed it to him.

"Sherrill it was nice meeting you, make sure you give me a call!"

"I will!"

He walked off to his friends, then they left out the restaurant. A bone white Cadillac Escalade pulled up. Two Mexicans hopped out, one open the door for Guardo, while the other stood guard. Guardo stirred at the one that open the door. "Did you see her in there?" Guardo asked.

"No boss!"

"Don't worry, if she still in this city, we will find her dead or alive."

"Damn this bitch good!" Dat thought to himself as he watched Sherrill mingling with the Mexican. He couldn't believe how she had already moved on to the next nigga before Tim even got found guilty. Dat didn't know the Mexican personally word on the street was he had the work by the boatload for the cheap. Dat was necking like a ma'fucka and he knew it. Only thing he was concerned about was getting cool with Sherrill so he could get hooked up with the Mexican, he kept his eyes focus on Sherrill like a hungry wolf.

Nina pulled up in a Q50 Infiniti, in Jaspers parking lot, the parked and hopped out. The temperature was in the high nineties. She and Dat spoke earlier and agreed to meet there for something to eat and some drinks. She was wearing a pair of high heeled stiletto pumps, a Karen Miller dress that rode her like a jockey on a horse at the Kentucky Derby. She walked into the filled beyond capacity room, in search of Dat. Her eyes sparkled with excitement after seeing Dat sitting at a table with an ice bucket with two bottles of Cristal, and a bottle of Dom Perignon, bobbing his head to the music.

Vedo stood next to him rocking a red and white National fitted cap, a red polo shirt, some polo jeans with a pair of red and white high top Prada sneakers. Nina pranced her happy ass over, Dat stood then wrapped his arms his arms around her waist, then his hand around her ass cheeks. He spun her around, then they began dancing. The whole time while they were dancing, Nina flirted with him, while Dat grinded on her. Finally they sat at the table and swallowed glass after glass of champagne. Dat was horny and was done with the flirting, he was ready to see if her sex game was like she claimed it was.

"No...Nina, how I know you not faking!" he slurred out.

Nina smiled then bit her lips. "Well I guess I have to show you!"

The club had died down and most of the patrons were either heading home or either going down Club Stadium. Dat was past wasted from consuming all the champagne, He has persuaded Nina into going to a hotel.

"Vedo....!" Bat shouted out, I..I...I'm fuck...fucked up., IMA need you to drive my shit!"

Vedo snickered after seeing how fucked up he was, he really didn't give a flying fuck, his mind was more on pushing the shit out of Dat Aston Martin. Dat and Nina came staggering out, arms around each other. Vedo laughed, thinking Dat was a wild ass nigga. Nina helped Dat inside of her Infiniti. Seconds later the Infiniti light came on. Vedo watched them pull off then started up the Ashton then went on his way.

30 Minutes Later

Dat was laying butt naked in a Days Inn Express. Nina stood topless, she stripped completely naked. Dat huffed when he saw how fat and pretty her pussy was. She motioned for him to come over. He crawled over stroking his dick in his hand. He didn't waste any time ramming his dick in her pussy, causing her to grit her teeth, while vigorously pounding his dick in her. Nina grunted with each stroke. Dat could see the pleasure expression on her face, Nina was humping back and forth, matching him stroke for stroke. Dat was loving every minute of it. Nina bent forward resting her head in the pillow, so she could allow him to go deeper, he dug his dick damn near in her chest!

"O God...Cum in me!" she pleaded.

Her pussy lips were wrapped around his dick like some vice grips. He tried his hardest to refrain from cumming, until he busted enough semen that could put out a wild fire. He fell on his back, Nina gently grabbed his dick, doing her best to stroke it back up. She took her tongue and licked the head then his balls.

"Th..There you go baby girl!" he stuttered encouraging her to continue. After his dick was back bone hard he rammed it down her throat. She sucked it causing her to cum.

"O shit!" he moaned feeling his toes curling up.

She continued to suck his dick like a porn star, sucking and slurping at the same time, as he nutted down her throat. She swallowed every drop. He pulled out then pushed her on the bed. She laid on her stomach. She loved it how he took control, she waited for him to ram his dick in her anal, but to her surprise he slid his tongue in there.

"Ow!" she panted out feeling the saliva and cum oozing down her thighs.

Once he finished, she had a smile on her face, from how he had her asshole feeling clean. She rested her head on his chest until the both fell asleep.

Dat woke up with a migraine headache, he rolled over. Nina was lying next to him legs spread eagle. Dat looked at her freshly shaved pussy lips, he buried his face between her legs and began running his tongue slowly up and down her clit, then he sucked it gently while slurping on her slimy wet juice. Nina was smiling enjoying the waves of pleasure. She began panting and moaning. Her clit had swollen twice its size. Dat continued sucking and massaging her pussy, to he moved down to her ass. She felt his wet slick tongue enter her booty hole.

"OH Dat!" she pleaded, rubbing his bald head.

She placed her fingers inside her soaking wet pussy, fingering herself for more pleasure. She pulled her fingers out sticking them in her mouth. Dat turned her over, then stuck his finger in her pussy, he pulled it out and gently inserted it in her asshole without warning. Then he rammed his dick in her ass, causing her body to jerk. She could feel him swell inside of her.

"Fuck the shit out of me Dat!"

"Fuck me back Nina!" Dat demanded

He didn't have to tell her twice. She started throwing her hips, he was enjoying himself fucking her ass like it was a pussy. He shot his semen up into her asshole, then let out a moan, after cumming in her. He pulled out in a bliss. They both dozed back off to sleep smelling like fresh sex.

Nina was laid next to Dat, butt naked, dead to the world. Her cell phone chirped causing Dat to wake. He woke up with an attitude he looked over toward the digital clock it read 9:45.

"Nina!" he shouted in Nina ear. "Get that fucking phone before I break that shit!"

Nina woke up groggily, looking at him like he was crazy, and then laid back down.

"Bitch you better answer the mufucker!"

She wanted badly to tell him to kiss her ass but he already done that.

"Damn Dat, I'm going to answer it, but you don't have to call me a bitch!" she said shocked how he was talking to her.

"Bitch who the fuck you think you fucking wit, I call you what the fuck I want to call you, bitch don't get fucked up!" he said with much attitude. He had no problem putting hands or feet on a bitch.

Nina was hotter than the Sahara Desert. She hopped out the bed, then grabbed her phone and clothes. She marched in the bathroom. She couldn't believe how she had just fucked him and now he disrespecting her like a bitch ass nigga. After the way he talked to her, made her appreciate Bubble more.

Niecy was up around 6:30 in the morning after her alarm clock went off. She set it to make sure she was woke in case Tim called. At 7:14 he called and they talked she was happy to hear from him. They discussed what he what he needed her to do.

"You miss me baby?" he asked.

"You know I do!"

"Alright baby after you leave the lawyer, make sure you pick up the phone."

"I gotchu!"

"I love you baby!"

"I love you more!"

The phone beeped then shut off. An hour later Niecy decided to pull out the Bentley coupe, she hadn't had the desire to drive it being that so much had been going on. After talking to Tim she felt better. She and Trina was flying up Indian head highway doing 110 mph, listening to a Mary J cd. Niecy looked over at Trina watching her absorb the fresh air. She slowed down after seeing a Maryland State Trooper cruising ahead. The last thing she wanted was to get pulled over or get arrested before she had a chance to take Trina to meet Tim lawyer Jennifer Wicks.

"Bitch that was close!" she thought happy as fuck she didn't get pulled over. They continued cruising up the highway, listening to Mary J. Trina was singing with the song way off beat, Niecy looked at her not believing how bad she was fucking the song up.

"Bitch who sing that song!" Niecy asked already knowing.

"Girl you know that's Mary!"

"Well bitch how bout letting Mary sing it then."

The two burst out laughing. Niecy was still laughing as she turned on the exit to Benning Road. She looked at her Cartier wristwatch, seeing how she had a little time to waist. She turned in the Hechinger Mall so she could stop at the Radio Shack, then she pulled out some Mac lip gloss. She looked in her rearview mirror checking to make sure she was still Diva upped.

"Trina I need you to get behind the wheel, I have to run in the store for a second, I'll be right back."

Trina didn't have a problem with it, in fact after riding in it she had thoughts of trading her 645 in for one. But in a different color. What she didn't know was she would never get a chance to buy one.

Guardo sat in the back seat waiting for Deuce, who went inside of the ice cream parlor for some ice cream. Guardo couldn't believe his eyes, he tapped Chico on shoulder. "Look over there!" he said pointing at Trina sitting in the driver's seat of the Bentley. Chico reached under his seat, pulling out a Taurus 9mmm, then clicked the safety making it ready to fire. He tucked it under his shirt, then hopped out the truck with plans on catching a body. He started off power walking, then slowed down, creeping upon his mark. Trina was so into the music, that she never saw the Taurus pointed

to her head. BLAKA..BLAK..BLAK..BLAK..BLAK.
Matter and the majority of Trina brains were
splattered on the windshield. Chico took off running
to a waiting running Cadillac. Then it sped off.

Niecy walked out the store wondering why there
was a crowd of people standing around her car.
She assumed that they were just admiring her car,
until she heard an elderly woman screaming and
shouting her head off. Niecy took off running to her
car. When she got there Trina was lying face down
on the steering wheel, with a hole in the back of
her head the size of a grape fruity. Niecy fell to the
ground crying as tears flowed from her face. The
police and the firemen and ambulance workers
arrived. The police blocked the area off with yellow
tape, making it a crime scene. The Coroner arrived
and announced Trina was dead.

Homicide Detective Stones and his partner
Detective Brown was questioning Niecy being that
she was the registered owner of the Bentley.
Stones had explained to her that her car was being
confiscated for evidence. Stone could tell that she
was still a little traumatized.

"Mrs. White... If you like we wouldn't have a
problem giving you a ride home if you need us to!"
he said in a friendly gesture.

"No thanks, I'll catch a cab." "This
motherfucker thinks he slicker than a mop at a gas

station, she thought to herself. She was fucked up, not enough to give them a chance to get her address. Even if they didn't get it from the car registration, but if they didn't they damn sure wasn't going to get it from her. She flagged a cab down then hopped in the back. She was about to grab her cell, until she realized she left it in the car. She told the drier Tim mother address, hoping he would call over there, she knew he probably had call her cell nonstop wondering why she wasn't there yet. She rode in silence the whole ride, as tears rolled down her eyes. The cab driver pulled in front of Tim mother house. She was sitting on the porch talking to a neighbor. When she saw Niecy getting out a cab, she assumed something wasn't right. Niecy started walking towards her with her a fist full of tears. Pat knew for sure something was wrong.

"Baby what's the matter?" she shouted grabbing Niecy hands. Niecy explained everything that happened as they walked into her house.

Tim was in his cell waiting to go on his visit, he looked at himself in the tiny mirror that was on the wall of his cell. After carefully checking himself over, he looked at his watch wondering what was taking Niecy so long. He decided he was going to call her cell. He walked out his cell and noticed a crowd of inmates huddled around a tv. He kept walking headed to make his call. He picked the phone up off the receiver then dialed Niecy cell. It rung a few times then went to voicemail.

"Where the fuck she at?" he thought after trying to call her again getting the voicemail.

He hung up the phone on the receiver, then walked over where Bigga and some inmates were huddled around the tv.

"Bigga what up with it!"

"Shit some broad just got smoked in the Hechinger Mall in a pink Bentley Coupe!"

Tim looked over toward the tv and his heart almost stopped.

"Good evening this is Cory Harris from Channel Five News. We are here at Hechinger Mall, where an African American female in her twenties was found shot to death in a pink Bentley Coupe in front of the Radio Shack. Witnesses say they saw a Latino male in his early twenties, around 6ft, 200lbs, running away from the scene. We will give you more details when they are available, this is Cory Harris from Channel Five News."

It took everything inside of him not to bust out the tv. He wiped the tears from his face, looking Bugga in the eyes. "Slim that was my girl!" he said as the tears rolled down his face. HE closed his eyes and said a quick prayer. Bigga stood and watched not knowing what to say. Tim dapped Bigga up, then walked off to his cell.

Hour Later

"KNOCK...KNOCK!"

Officer Field was standing at the door of Tim's cell.. "Hello Mr. Gamble, I'm sorry to disturb you." she could see he was crying. "How you feeling?" He looked towards her. "I....already know!"

Her heart went out to him knowing it was already hard for him being away from loved ones, now finding out that one of them had been murdered. "Well when you get yourself together, the chaplain needs to see you in his office!"

"Yea alright!"

Tim mind was racing a hundred miles a minute. Everyone he loved was dead, at that moment if he could have traded his life to bring them back he would have. A few minutes later he went to the chaplain's office. With only making a few free direct phone calls, it was known that the chaplain would allow an inmate who had just recently lost a family member or loved one, a phone call or two. Tim wasn't in the mood to be hearing no long sympathetic conversation I'm sorry for your loss she in a better place bullshit. If he did, he was going tell the chaplain to take his phone call and ram it in his ass.

"Hello Mr. Gamble, I hear you already know why you're here." Tim shook his head in agreement.

"Your mother had called and she would like you to give her a call."

Tim took a seat, the chaplain passed him his desk phone. Tim immediately dialed his mother phone.

"Mom!"

"Tim... baby you alright?"
"Yea mom, I'm good."

"Tim hold on for a second." she passed the phone to Niecy.

"Tim!" Niecy shouted thru the phone.

Hearing her voice was like hearing sweet music. He had a smile on his face, there were tears of joy rolling down his cheeks.

"Oh my God, Niecy baby I thought you was gone!"

"Baby I'm... alright... but Trina dead baby!" she said between crying.

"Niecy what happened?"

"Tim we were on our way to meet your lawyer, and I stopped at Radio Shack to get the phone you asked me to get. I left Trina in the car, then I went in the store and when I came out somebody killed her.

"Shit!" he shouted banging his fist against the desk, not caring how the chaplain felt. The chaplain looked at him, letting him know to watch his language. Niecy told him that the chaplain will allow her to have a special visit for the next day. He told Niecy to tell his mother he loved her and he was going to call them once he got back to his unit. He hung up then thanked the chaplain, then walked back to his unit.

He walked into his unit, relieved Niecy was alive, but still sad that Trina was not. As he walked to his cell he spotted a faggot name Jermaine that goes by the name Nicki Minaj, walking out his cell, with an ass fatter than some of the females that be in the latest Straight Stuntin magazine. Tim wasn't on no homosexual shit, and was hoping his celly wasn't either. He walked straight passed Nicki, without making any kind of eye contact, he walked in his cell, his celly James was standing over the toilet taking a piss.

"Hey celly, I need to holla at you when you finish!" Tim said then walked to the outside of the cell, thinking to himself, if this nigga was into some ole faggot shit, somebody had to go, and it damn sure wasn't going to be him.

"What up celly?" James asked.

"Look here homes, I don't give a fuck how you take this, I'm not saying you either or, I don't cell with faggots or hot niggas, so I'm going to step out the cell for a minute and if you either one of the two, by the time I come back, you need to pack your shit, and find you somewhere to go, or we gonna have a problem!"

Tim didn't know for sure which one James was, and really didn't give a flying fuck, but by the way James looked, and didn't respond back he knew it was one of them.

Tim sat on the tier watching the other inmates interact with each other playing chess, spades and dominoes. If you didn't know him you would've thought he was antisocial. He was never the type to interact with a lot of people, if he fucked with you, you would've known it. There was nothing he wouldn't do for you if he could.

"Hello Mr. Gamble, how you feeling?" Officer Fields asked knowing that he just lost a family member.

He looked over at her and smiled. She wasn't his type, but being locked up would have you looking at female officers like a stalker. DC jail inmates were known for flashing their private parts out on any female that was in their vicinity.

"I'm cool, how are you Mrs. Fields?" he asked looking at her looking real gullible.

"I'm good, I can't wait to get off!"

"What you going out on a date?" Tim asked trying to break the ice before running his spill, he has already peeped how she was gawking when he first walked in the unit. She even was watching him using Bigga phone at will, knowing he had to be somebody out in the mean DC streets, she knew that Bigga only allowed his crew to use his phone. If they weren't using it, it would just sit on the receiver as it was broke, while there were lines of inmates waiting to use the other phones.

"Naw I'm going out to see Wale and Backyard Band!"

He looked at her with a smile not believing she was the type that went out to the go-go. She was skinny and long, like a number 2 pencil, she kept her hair in braids, she had some nice juicy lips, what had her looking unattractive was her bent up Nike boots, that made her feet look like rollerblades.

"O yeah!" he answered looking away from her boots.

"Alright Mr. Gamble, I have to make my rounds."

"Alright Mrs. Field I'll holla at chu!"

As Officer Field walked off James came walking towards him with some papers in his hands.

"Celly can I speak to you for a minute?"

"Yea what's up?"

"Slim I want you to check my paperwork out." he said passing his transcripts.

"Slim I never told on nobody in my life, I just wanted you to know I'm not a rat, before I move out!"

He didn't have to say no more, if he wasn't a rat her a homo. Tim respected the fact he brought his paperwork, showing he wasn't a rat but he still had to go.

"Look slim I'm not one to judge you, but you already know you got to go, but you been cool with me since I moved here, so as long as you do you and don't include me we can still be cool!"

"Alright!" James said feeling relieved. "I already found a cell to move in so I'm gonna go head and pack my shit."

"Cool." Tim said.

Officer Field was walking toward Tim looking like a sheet of paper, Tim assumed she was in reference to James moving.

"Mr. Gamble you have a legal visit."

"Alright."

When he entered the visiting room, Jennifer Wicks his lawyer were already there reading from some papers.

"Hey Jen, what's good?"

She looked up I have some good news and some bad."

"Come on with it."

"Well first the bad, you might have to sit here for a while, the prosecutor trying to paint you as a cold blooded killer. Now the good, I got a call from Rome Jones lawyer, telling me before Trina was murdered she had went and wrote a signed confession to murdering her husband, and how she gave you the gun. I had an investigator to do a little research and the gun came back with Trina prints on the trigger with partial prints from you. Now I'm going to get the murder thrown out, and as far as the drug case, the only person that could have hurt you was Rome. Trina really saved your ass!" Tim smiled with excitement, and here he thought she set him up.

"Alright Tim, I'm going go and get on top of everything, I'm going see you next week, for a bond hearing. Hopefully you can keep clean by staying out of trouble."

"I will, and I'm going have Niecy drop your money off."

"Yeah I was about to get around to that." she said with a smile. Her face was red like a beet, she was cool as shit to be a white girl.

Sherrill was double parked in front of the DC Jail. Lee was in the back seat with her son lil Moody, looking like his dad, wearing a polo short set and fresh pair of Jordan's.

"Lee tell Moody if he see Tim, tell him to give me a call."

"Bitch I don't know why you still thinking about his ass, I know you liked him, but that nigga about to get an ass full of time. I wouldn't be surprised if they don't send his ass to the ADX. If I was you, I'll be concentrating on that fine ass Mexican from Jaspers. That look like he was caked up to."

"Well hooker I'm not you!" Sherrill snapped. Sherrill now knew why Moody wanted to beat her ass, when he came home. Sherrill and Lee were like sisters, but their morals were definitely different.

"Sherrill I'm just saying!"

"Bitch just stay out my business, I don't judge you, so don't judge me!"

Niecy stood in line watching damn near the same people that was there to visit their loved one the last time she was there. She was looking at a female holding a little boy around three. Niecy smiled at the kid while thinking to herself that if she would've gotten pregnant, that could have been her bringing her baby to visit Tim. After being searched, Niecy sat in the visiting room waiting for Tim to walk in the room. A couple of minutes later he walked in wearing an orange jumpsuit. She picked up the phone while still looking him over. He still had a swag about him, still looking immaculate as ever, even in a jail outfit.

He picked up the phone then smiled back.

"How you doing baby?" she asked

"I'm cool other than missing you."

"I miss you more."

As they talked, she told him everything about Trina being murdered, how Trina told her she had cremated Rome body, then tossed him in the ocean. She wanted badly to tell him about his father, but she knew that wasn't her place. He told everything his lawyer told him. They talked for a while until the guard walked up and told Tim that their visit was coming to an end. They sat the remainder of the visit, staring in each other eyes tracing their fingers on the glass that separated them. While telling each other how much they loved the other. Tim stood and blew Niecy a kiss, as he was leaving. He spotted Lee and a lil kid he assumed was Moody son, being that he looked just like Moody. Moody walked in and gave Tim a handshake like they were two old friends. Tim wanted badly to tell him to tell Lee to let Sherrill know he inquired about her, but he didn't want to chance Niecy finding out. Niecy was all he wanted, he would have given anything he could to take back the hurt he caused her, he wanted Niecy to be able to trust him and for her to know he loved only her.

Guardo was standing in a warehouse, watching Ace and Chico and four other Mexicans load bundles of cocaine inside of a specially equipped van that was used for hiding and transporting large quantities of cocaine. After being satisfied with the way the cocaine was carefully hidden Guardo walked off into his office and shut the door. He had everything that a man would need and want, except a woman to share the things he had. He could have any woman his heart desire. He never found the desire until he sat eyes on Sherrill. He couldn't keep his mind off her. He reached in his pocket pulling out his cell, then scrolled down his contact list then pressed in a few numbers and waited until someone answered on the other end.

"Hello." the female voice on the other end said.

"Hola como estas?" (how are you)

"Actually I feel much better after hearing your voice.

"Well we gonna have to start calling each other more often, we can't have you feeling bad... You know my girlfriend and I was having a conversation about you earlier."

"Is that so?"

"Yeah she thought you were handsome."

"And you?"

"And me what?" she asked not picking up on him inquiring about what she thought about his looks.

"Do you think I'm handsome?"

"Actually I do"

"Well Sherrill, I haven't done this in quite some time, but I would like if you allow me to take you out to a nice restaurant of your choice, so I can get a chance to get to know you."

"Sure." she said excitedly.

"Well how about you set up a reservation and give me a call back,"

"Guardo do you eat steak?" she asked hoping he wasn't a vegetarian.

"Actually I love steak!"

"You too!" she said under her breath. Well Guardo I know this nice restaurant by the Capitol.

Guardo pulled in front of Charlie Palmer restaurant in the Capitol Hill area, downtown DC, in a black tinted out Audi A8, he hopped out the luxury fully equipped vehicle wearing a white Hugo Boss crush linen suit, with a black Hugo hard sole loafers. Chico and Deuce sat across the street, eyes trained on him, in a rental, hunch low in their seat, each with their hands clutched around a fully equipped assault weapon. Guardo passed his keys to the valet worker, then walked inside the restaurant. He looked around the restaurant until his eyes spotted

Sherrill sitting at the bar. She had her dreads freshly done, she was wearing a sweater and skirt from Michael Kors, a pair of Jimmy Choo pumps, sipping on a glass of Moe-Moe So. Guardo walked up behind her.

"Hello handsome!" she said with a bright smile on her face, extending her right hand out.

"Hello beautiful!" he said in a soft silky voice, while clutching her hands inside of his. He roamed his eyes up and down her body. She was attractive by any definition. The maitre'd walked over, with a pen and pad.

"Two for dinner?" he asked

"Yes." Sherrill answered for the both of them.

He escorted the two to a table, in the back of the restaurant in a secluded area.

"Your waitress will be with you in a moment."

A few minutes later the waitress came back and took their order.

The food from Charlie Palmer was excellent, Sherrill had the surf and turf, Guardo had crab cakes and fries. The two set and drank red wine. Guardo waved over the waitress and ordered a bottle of

Louie. He looked Sherrill in her eyes, it's been two years since he spent quality time with a female, ever since losing his wife to a car accident. He was finally ready to start enjoying being with a woman.

"Thank you Sherrill, for allowing me the opportunity to enjoy myself with such a beautiful woman!"

She smiled damn the nigga say all the sweetest thing and fine as hell! She thought to herself.

The waitress brought back the bottle of Louie. After tossing back shot after shot of Louie Sherrill knew then why people spent $100 a shot for Louie. She was feeling light headed, she was twisted out her mind, drunker than a skunk! Guardo knew he could have had his way with her, sex wasn't what he was after, he wanted her heart. He glanced at his presidential Rolex. After observing how intoxicated she was. He looked her deep in her eyes.

"Sherrill would you like to order a dessert?"

"Sure!"

He smiled at her enjoying the moment, out of all the beautiful Latino women he have had, he loved a African American woman.

"Sherrill I think we should be leaving, as bad as I don't want to end this date, I think it's best for now." he said being that alcohol was the cause of him looking in his eyes.

"Thank you!" he whispered.

The waitress brought the dessert back, Guardo told her to pack them in separate to go bags. After Guardo paid the bill, they left out and walked to the valet area. Sherrill was fumbling inside her purse in search of her parking ticket. "Damn I'm fucked up!" she said.

Guardo smiled then started feeling bad he allowed her to get so wasted. Chico and Deuce kept their eyes on the pair like they were secret service. A couple minutes later the valet workers pulled up with their cars. Sherrill thanked Guardo for dinner, then kissed him on his cheek.

"Sherrill make sure you call me when you get home." he said.

"I will."

Sherrill drove home, knowing that the next time she went out with Guardo, if she enjoyed herself like she had, instead of him giving her some dessert after dinner, he would be giving her some dick. She pulled up to her building, then got out of her car, staggering in her building.

"Hey Sherrill, what up with it?" Meechi her next door neighbor said.

Meechi was what you call a pretty boy, a little thuggish, pitch black with jet black wavy hair, the way she liked her men. Meechi could see she been out getting her drink by the way she was wobbling.

Sherrill laughed him off, knowing he wanted to fuck her. A couple times she thought about giving him some pussy, but she was too cool with his wife. She stuck her key in her door. As soon as she got inside, she took off her clothes, stripping down to her bra and panties. Her head was still spinning from the drinks. She dove on her sofa, within seconds she found herself with her fingers inside her pussy, she began licking her lips, while gently rubbing her clit, with each climax she moaned with pleasure. She sexed herself with her finger to she came before falling asleep.

Homicide Detective Stones and his partner Homicide Detective Brown was sitting at a desk in the homicide room, looking over some evidence. Vice Squad Detective Trina Johnson walked in the room a sec later unannounced.

"Hello Gentlemen!" speaking to the both of them, while looking over at Brown, knowing he had a little crush on her. She stuck her hands out to Brown that was surprisingly firm and muscular. If she only knew as soon as their hands met, Brown dick stood at attention. He tried his best to keep from lurking his eyes on her body. Her ass and breast was bursting out the Marc Jacobs skirt and blouse she was wearing. He turned his eyes away from her body, down to her freshly done pedicured toes, that was sticking out a pair of Tihi stilettoes.

"Have a seat Detective." Stone said nodding his head in the direction of the chair.

She sat then crossed her legs with a sexual smile on her face.

"So Johnson what brings you around homicide?" Stone asked.

She cleared her throat then explained how she felt Trina murder was a hit, and how she had an idea who was behind it. She told them, it wasn't a coincidence that Trina was murdered in the fiancé car, of the man who was charged with killing her husband.

"Uh huh!" Stone grumbled. "So you thinking that the fiancé, knows more than she telling us.

"No question!", Johnson replied. "Well gentlemen, I'm not gonna hold y'all up. I just wanted to stop by before Mrs. White got a chance to skip town." she said shooting a symbolical message.

She stood up wiping her hands on her back end, then sashayed out the door knowing Detective Brown would be watching her ass.

"So Stone what you think, you think she on something?"

"Brown, bad as I hate to admit it, she might be right, we gonna have to put a tag on Mrs. White and get a warrant from a judge so we could tap her phone.

Bubble was standing in front of his shop. Nina and the kids had just pulled off. He had just finished lining his son TJ hair, while Nina and their daughter Tini got manicures and pedicures. Nina had told Bubble she was taking the kids out to a buffet, to get them something to eat, and then to a movie, trying to play the good wife. If only Bubble knew she was a slut, whore, liar and a goddamn thief. She should have been serving time for all the money she stole from him. Bubble loved his family more than anything in the world. He lived and breathed for them. He wanted to take his family on a summer vacation. But money was low. He was barely making enough to cover his bills, with school about to start and the kids needing school clothes and supplies. Between him and Nina hitting his saving he was going broke. He was thinking to himself beating himself up knowing that he had to make a move. Knowing he wouldn't be able to cut hair much longer with old age and bad health.

Visions of Nina appeared in his head of her fucking around with other men. He used to see how she looked at young men that came into his shop. He began thinking back to the days back in New York when he was making stupid money. He reached in his pants pocket and pulled out his wallet then begin searching it until he found a card he got from an old friend, from New York he ran into one day, while he was at a carwash getting his car clean. He looked over at the building they call the Carter, with lust in his eyes. He felt if things went the way he had planned, he would be able to take his family on a vacation and stack up some money. His plan was to get some money or die trying.

A Week Later

It didn't take Bubble long to recruit a crew of hustlers willing to help him get the Carter back in motion. He had paid a few crack heads to cut the grass and pick up all the trash around the building. He did everything to make the wore down building look more presentable. Only thing that was missing was a sign that read, Open Under New Management!

With the good coke he had coped, he had the carter open like a 7-11. When he first met his new connect he was out selling rocks in a building that Bubble ran. A couple of Bubble workers caught him in the building slinging rocks after he was warned not to. They robbed him of his drugs and money and held him to Bubble arrived. The little bit of drugs he had on him wasn't enough to have affected Bubble cash flow. Bubble felt he had to deal with the younging for no more than the principle and to send a message to all who had thought about coming in there hustling. When Bubble arrived his two workers had their pistol pointed to his head. Seeing the way the youngster stood and looked in the eye like a man, who was willing to accept his fate, Bubble wanted to know what would make him play with his life. If he would say the wrong thing, the next conversation that was said about him would've been in the past tense. Realizing his life could come to an end, the young Mexican spoke in perfect English.

"Sir I'm sorry and it won't happen again, I was just trying to make some money to pay the rent for my family. My father was sent back to Mexico and me and my mother were left here."

Bubble looked him over. "What your name boy?"

"Guardo"

"Look hear kid, the only reason you're not dead right now, I respect you willing to risk your life to help your family. But if I ever hear about you slinging rocks up in here and they're not from me, that will be your life, you understand!"

"Yes!"

Bubble let out a lil chuckle, thinking how much Guardo reminded him of himself when he was around that age. "This lil motherfucker have a lot of balls!" From that moment they built a relationship. With the help of Bubble, Guardo turned out to be one of the youngest millionaires in New York. Even before hooking up with an uncle that was one of Mexico's biggest drug cartel.

Dat pulled up across the street then parked, with plans on taking over where Tim left off. His hood Potomac Gardens had been shut down the last few days. The feds was posted 24/7 around the entire projects. Before Tim was arrested the Carter used to bring in at least $20-30,000 a day in rock sells. If you would have added weight, there was no telling what was made. All Dat had to do now was find a connect. He still had around $100,000 of his money not including the $150,000 he owed Tim. He had to make something happen, especially the way he liked to ball out of control., he was known to blow money faster than a crackhead go thru a welfare check on the first of the month.

Images of Sherrill was floating in his head of her helping him get set up with the Mexican who had the good coke for the cheapest price in town. Dat looked over at the Carter, carefully watching two young dudes, looking like they were slinging their product. He had to talk himself out of getting out and running them off. He knew after he got some work, if he had to get on some gorilla shit with the youngsters, either they was gonna get down or get laid down.

The next morning around noon, Sherrill woke up completely naked and her head ached. Even worse her stomach felt like it was full of anthrax. "Aw shit!" she moaned. She could hear her cell ringing from her purse she had hoped it would stop, but it continued. She reached and pulled it out her purse.

"Hello." she said in a groggy voice.

"Sherrill what you doing?" Lee asked.

"Come on bitch, not right now!" Sherrill replied agitated.

"Excuse me for checking up on you!"

"Lee girl my fucking head is killing me."

The phone line beeped. "Lee hold on a sec." Sherrill clicked over.

"Hello."

"Good morning Sherrill, or should I say good evening?" Guardo said sounding extra cheerful.

She cleared her throat and instantly her headache magically disappeared. "Hello Guardo." she replied with a bright smile gracing her lips, her arms and legs were covered with goose bumps.

"I just called to make sure you were alive, being that you hadn't called me letting me know you made it home safe."

"I apologize... please forgive me, I came home and fell the fuck out!"

"No apology is needed, just knowing you made it home safe is enough." They both could hear Sherrill other line hanging up.

"Forgive me Sherrill, I didn't mean to interrupt you."

"Don't worry about it, she'll call back." Sherrill said not caring that Lee hung up. She really didn't feel like talking to her anyway, she would have rather talk to him instead.

"Well Sherrill I'm going to let you go, but if you find some time late today, give me a call."

"I sure will."

Niecy and Tim mother was sitting in the courtroom. Nothing in the world would have prevented them from being there. The courtroom was jammed packed, that they had to stop allowing people from entering. There was a section designated for the press. This case was one of the biggest high profile cases the city has seen since the Rayful Edmonds, Tony Lewis, Wayne Perry, Tim Gray and Rodney Moore case. Tim was escorted in from the back of the courtroom. He was looking cooler than a cucumber. He was seated next to his lawyer. The marshal that brought him in stood a few feet behind them. Jennifer was watching the geeky looking prosecutor that look like he was fresh out of law school. After seeing him, Jennifer felt Tim odds of receiving bond just got better. She was expecting USDA Officer Phyllis Johnson, being she was on the best DA's in her office.

Detective Johnson walked in then took a seat behind the prosecutor desk. Tim glanced over toward her. There wasn't much of a discernible reaction from him. Judge Bates walked in from the back of the courtroom with a stack of papers in his hands. The bailiff ordered everyone in the courtroom to rise.

"Good morning everyone, you all may be seated." Judge Bates said as he sat down.

"Are we prepared to go forward this morning?"

"Mr. West?"

"Government is ready!"

"Mrs. Wicks?"
"Yes your honor, we are ready!"

"All right we're here today for a hearing for a bond for Mr. Gamble. For the court's record we have a criminal action 16-215 United States vs. Tim Gamble. We have Dennis West representing the government, Mrs. Jennifer Wicks representing the defendant and Shelly Brock representing probation.

"Mr. West you can begin!"

"Your honor the government is here today to show why Mr. Gamble should be held without bond, he said looking over his notes. Mr. Gamble is being charged with possession of a firearm that was used to murder a government informer, Mr. Rome Jones, who had just testified that Mr. Gamble was involved in the murder of another informant Richard Putt Lee, who was murdered in Atlanta, Georgia. Who was scheduled to testify against Mr. Gamble. Also Mr. amble, is a suspect in the murders of five people that were gunned down in the Trinidad area on Orlean Place." He took a seat as if he has just made the winning shot in a basketball game. Jennifer stood up like a boxer that been knocked down, she refused to be outdone by an up and coming prosecutor, she was ready to welcome him to the big league and free her client at the same time.

"First your honor I want to say everything that the government claims against my client are false and hearsay, except he was in possession of the gun that was used to murder Mr. Gamble."

The courtroom was in awe, shocked to hear her admit that Tim had the gun that killed Rome.

"Your honor I have a DNA expert that is going to testify that the gun found on Mr. Gamble had the prints of Mrs. Trina Jones. There were only partial prints belonging to Mr. Gamble. I will also call the attorney for Mr. and Mrs. Jones that has a signed confession that states Mrs. Jones has admitted murdering her husband." Jennifer was revved up.

She began laying it on thick. Mr. Gamble and Mr. Jones had been best friends since they were kids, not only were they best friends, Mr. Gamble was Mr. Jones best man at his wedding. And Mr. Jones was to be Mr. Gamble's best man at his wedding this summer. Jennifer took a seat, then winked her eye at the sexy young prosecutor. Judge Bates ordered Mr. West and Jennifer to approach the bench. He had told them he was going to call a recess, he needed to go over the signed confession before he decided to allow it or not to allow it to be used as evidence.

30 Minutes Later

The Judge allowed Harry Tutt to the stand and testified on behalf of the defense. He was sworn in then testified how Trina came to his office and made and wrote a signed confession. He went on and explained how Trina said she shot and killed Rome because he was beating her.

"Object!" Mr. West shouted

"Overruled!" Judge Bates replied.

Jennifer was satisfied with her witness, knowing without him, Tim was looking at a life sentence without parole. She had a surprise that she kept to herself knowing that it was far from over.

The judge ordered the case for a continuance to the following Friday. Detective Johnson wasn't happy with the way the motion was going. She wanted Tim to be found guilty of all charges and sent away in a penitentiary with a life sentence. She had to this case personally. She wanted him to rot in prison more than she had ever had for no other. She stood up and rushed out the courtroom with a vanilla envelope in her hand. When Niecy walked out the courtroom into the lobby, she spotted Detective Johnson standing staring in her direction. Niecy shot her a hateful stare from across the hallway.

"If this bitch come over here with some bullshit. I'm going to get arrested for beating her ass!" she thought to herself.

Detective Johnson walked over. "Mrs. White may I speak to you for a second?"

"Mrs. White, I know we met on some bad terms but I was only doing my job. I have something I think you might find interesting."

Niecy stood silent as Detective Johnson handed her a folder, Niecy opened the folder, then pulled out a stack of pictures of Tim and Sherrill at Rome party. She had thought she had seen enough until she saw the pictures of Tim kissing Trina. Here she was missing and mourning about the same bitch that was kissing and Lord knows what else she was doing with her man. She slammed the photos to the ground, then walking off not saying a word. After seeing how Niecy reacted Detective Johnson knew it wouldn't take long before Niecy would break and eventually leave Tim and turn her back on him like so many women have done after finding out their man have cheated on her after he got arrested.

Tim and the other inmates were about to get on the bus that took inmates back to jail.

"Hey Robinson... Put Gamble on the van!"

Tim looked back trying to figure out what was going on.

"LT what's going on?" Tim asked

"Just look at it like you a personal chauffeur!" LT said as if her said something slick.

"So you wouldn't mind if he take me to get some pussy?"

"O you definitely going where there's a whole lot of pussy, if you like male pussy!" he said laughing at his own joke.

"LT you going to play with me like that, when we get there!" Tim said not one to allow anyone to disrespect him.

"Motherfucker, you may run shit in the street, but I run shit up around here nigger!"

"LT you not afraid to talk to me like that!"

Tim had plans on dealing with the LT once the right time presented itself. Officer Robinson help Tim in the van, not wanting to be a part of none of that.

Tim was ready to get back to the jail so he could call Niecy, get something to eat, and take a shower. The van pulled inside the jail, Officer Robinson had orders to rush Tim inside the jail.

"Damn Robinson, what's up with all this?"

"Gamble I don't know what's going on, I'm just following orders."

Bunny and Nina brother Jerry was riding up Bladensburg Rd, while Bunny 12 year old son TJ was snoozing in the back seat of the Cadillac. Dat pulled up on the right of the cadi, in a stolen tinted caravan, Vedo rolled his window down ready to kill everybody inside the cadi. He stuck a glock .45 with an extended clip out the window. **BOC...BOC...BOC...BOC...BOC...BOC..** was the sound coming from the large automatic weapon. The large slugs caused Bunny to swerve the cadi, making it crash into a fire hydrant causing water to flood into the street. Dat hit the throttle peeling off like a bat outta hell. He had a devilish deranged look on his face. He made a sharp right turn on L street. It didn't take long before he spotted his next vics, conversing with each other, while smoking a blunt.

Vedo hopped out the van, like a lion in search of his prey. The tallest of the two spotted Vedo creeping up on them. He could see the bulge under Vedo sweatshirt. A knot of fear was in his gut, his partner turned around and was immediately terrified. Before they could react, Vedo popped off hitting both men with slugs to their head, dropping both men like a bag of bricks. Vedo took off running, with the smoking gun in hand, then hopped in the van. Dat hit the gas causing the causing the van to speed off, fishtailing up the block. Crack head John had just finish taking a shit in the bushes, and saw the whole event go down.

*****

Homicide Detective was standing over talking to a fellow officer, when his partner pulled up. There were fire trucks, ambulances and one third of the fifth district police force were there on the scene. Homicide Detective Brown looked over toward the bullet ridden cadi that looked like swiss cheese. It had so many holes in it that it looked as if it was used for target practice. Brown walked over to his partner.

"Any casualty Stones?" Brown asked.

"Yeah a goddamn 12 year old kid!"

"Oh my God what the fuck is this world coming to!" Brown said...."Where are the parents?"

Stones looked over then pointed toward a crying Bunny trying to get a last look at his lil man before the coroner carried him away to the morgue in a body bag. Brown shook his head, seeing the way Bunny was taken his son death, Brown could only imagine how the mother was going to take it.

Nina was in the kitchen, cooking dinner, singing love and war a Tamar Braxton song. "You go girl!" Nina said then laughed thinking how she and Tamara had come up. The two had a money tree, a fat man with lots of money. Things were looking up for Nina again. Bunny had been bringing in big bucks, he had given her money for the kid's school clothes and supplies, and an additional ten thousand to book a trip for her and the kids to go to Florida to Disney World. He even begin letting her shop and pick out his gear. They say if you clean up a gorilla, dress him in some nice clothes and out a lot of money in his pocket, he'll look just like a big black baller.

Tina Nina's 14 year old daughter was in the living room watching TV.

"Mom..mom!" Tina screamed....

"Tina!" Nina shouted before taking off running in the room checking on her.

"Mommie... somebody killed TJ!" she cried sobbing.

"What!.... Oh God...no...Please Lord, not my baby!"

Nina fell to her knees, wishing that she was having a bad dream. She snatched her cell from her hip then punched in Bunny number. "Bunny...where is my baby?"

It took everything in him to muster up the words. "Baby he gone!"

Rell and his crew drove thru Potomac gardens, ready to cash in on the $100,000 for Dat and Veto life. They had spent half the night looking for them, coming up empty.

"Kill moe on everything, I can't wait to smoke them niggers!" Rell said after pulling off seeing how the police and national guards had the whole project all hands on deck. Rell pulled out his cell, then made a call to his sister baby father Cruddle, who lived in the garden. Rell had a short conversation with him then promised to meet up with him later and pay him $5000 for the information he gave. He hated the fact he had to break bread with him. "Fuck it $95,000....$100,000 shit about the same." he thought to himself.

"What it do?" Trey Eight asked seeing the smile on Rell face.

"I got fool wifey address!" Rell said with a sly smirk on his face.

"Kill!" Trey Eight shouted/

"Ty you ready!" Rell asked.

"Ain't no secret!' she shouted from the back seat of the rental. While playing with a desert eagle.

She wanted to get it over with so she could get her cut then get back to the female she left at her apartment. Who pussy she ate and damn near fucked to death with a 10 inch dildo.

Erica Dat ex-wife lived in Laurel, MD. A nice community with mostly white people and quiet streets. She was a hard working secretary for the IRS. A faithful churchgoer. Rosedale Rell, Trey Eight and Ty sat in front of her house in the rental. Rell and Trey Eight. Tucked their pistol underneath their shirt then hopped out the rental and casually walked up toward the house, looking around making sure there was no one out.

They both lined up on the side of the house, then Ty hopped out wearing a big church hat and dress that had her looking like a preacher wife. She walked up to the door and rung the bell. A few seconds later Erica peeped thru the peephole, then opened the door. She didn't get a chance to say a word. Ty hit her in the mouth knocking her off her feet,, when she looked up Ty was pointing a desert eagle in her face. Rell and Trey Eight rushed in then shut the door behind them. Erica looked up at Ty, and started crying.

"What's going on?" she asked not knowing why the trio was in her house pointing guns at her. "Please don't kill me!"

Rell grabbed her by her hair. "Look bitch where the fuck is Dat!"

"I...I...don't know I swear!" she answered as tears were flowing down her face. Erica was past frightened. "I haven't talked to him since he called a couple days ago, telling me he was moving out of town!"

"Did he say where he was going?" Rell asked.

"No!"

Tynika was staring at her right breast that slid out her blouse. Rell had heard enough.

"Kill on my mama bitch if you call the police your ass will be good as dead!"

Erica exhaled relieved that they wasn't going to kill her. Rell nodded his head letting his crew know it was time to go.

"Come on we out!"

They all left out. Erica waited until she heard the vehicle the trio hopped inside, pull off before moving. She had told Dat that the things he did in the streets, would someday come back to hurt her.

"I ain't worried bout nothing....I ain't worried bout nothing....." Dat sung while driving up I 95 North headed up to New York with intention of finding a connect, then slide down Club 40/40 to get his freak on, with a model type broad. He was done with DC. He had paid Vedo $30,000, $10,000 for each body. The cruddy nigga he was, he thought about not paying for lil TJ body, being that TJ was just an innocent casualty. He knew not to play around with Vedo when it came to his money Vedo didn't play no games. Word in the street was that he had killed the pastor at his family church for misuse of the church money, the same man that baptized him when he was a kid. After pulling in the Ramada Hotel, Dat looked down at his diamond our Cartier sport watch. He had plans of taking a quick shower and a lil nap. His cell shook violently on his hip. He grabbed it, then looked down at the ID.

"What the fuck she want!" he thought to himself after seeing his ex-wife number, especially after their last conversation.

"Yea!" he answered nonchalantly

"Dat...What fuck u did!"

"Wha..what u talking about?"

"Nigga you know what the fuck I'm talking about! You have niggas running in my house pointing guns, looking for your stuttering ass! I hope you die bitch!" she shouted thru the phone before hanging up in his ear. She was speaking out of anger, but she meant every word. Even though he was a self-centered, cold hearted individual. He would never be able to live with himself if he was the cause of Erica being hurt. He loved her deeply, together or not, in his mind she would always be wifey. If it wasn't for the fact that he was so deep in the streets and into all the different freaks and whores he loved having wild sex with. He and Erica would still be together.

Instantly his pressure shot sky high, it felt like his brain was about to pop out his head. He grabbed his cell, then tried calling Vedo cell, hoping he wasn't running his mouth, if he was Dat had no problem putting money on his head. He hung up after Vedo cell went to voicemail. He had thought about turning around, then decided to rest up before heading back to DC. As he pulled in the hotel parking lot, he had a bad feeling in his stomach, after noticing a swarm of unmarked police cars They boxed him in, while the guest and bystanders rushed and scrambled to get a better view.

"What the fuck!" Dat thought as the door to the unmarked car open with officer hoping out pointing fully loaded assault weapons at him. He knew he was on his way to jail, after seeing FBI on their jacket. He was ordered out of his car, and was forced face down. A big redneck looking officer cuffed his hands behind him. The officer shouted in his ear.

"You are under arrest, you have the right to an attorney, anything you say can and will be used against you in a court of law, you have the right to remain silent, you understand your rights!'

He didn't wait for a response, he forced Dat into the back seat of one of the unmarked cars. Dat didn't know what he was getting arrested for, what he did know by the way the other officers were searching his car, he was never going to get to spend the $200,000 in his trunk.

Later that Evening

Homicide Detective Stone and his partner Brown walked in an interrogation room in a NY police station, where Dat was seated cuffed to a chair. When Dat saw the two officers he damn near shitted in his pants. He recognized Stone as soon as he saw his face. Stone was the leading officer on the case that resulted in his brother receiving a life sentence without parole...

"Mother….fucking..D…D….Dat!" Stone said smiling. "You stuttering motherfucker, you know you fucked up right!"

Detective Brown pulled up a seat beside Dat chair, he knew things wasn't looking good for Dat.

"Save yourself!" Brown said

Dat held to the code of honor, he didn't say a word, he was a lot of things but a rat wasn't one. He grew up in the era when men took the good with the bad, excepted the life they chose and choices they made.

"Browne fuck this piece of shit, I'm make sure his black ass receive a life sentence along with his brother."

"Fuck you pig!" Dat snarled with spit clinging on his lips.

"Cool out Stone!" Brown said to his partner. "Dat want you help us and we'll help you out!"

The two detectives stood up and walked out the room, leaving Dat to himself cuffed to the chair.

Next Day

It was a nice day out, cruddy was out bright and early, wearing a wife beater and a pair of skinny jeans, smoking a blunt of Kush, trapping sitting on

310

a bench on the basketball court. He refused to allow the police presence stop his cash flow. He noticed Cedo walking up with his peripheral vision.

"What up playboy?" Cruddy asked with an attitude.

Instead of speaking, Vedo burst out laughing, amazed and astonished how he was wearing skinny jeans, tighter than a virgin pussy.

"Fuck so funny!" Cruddy as with an attitude.

"Nigga you and them tight ass jeans!"

"Whatever nigga!"

Vedo could see that Cruddy was in his feeling. "Nigga fuck all that bullshit, what's up with that weed?"

"Ain't shit up with this weed, you wild ass nigger!"

Vedo continue laughing, not caring how he was feeling. Cruddy had a plan in his head for Vedo, they didn't call him Cruddy for nothing.

"Vedo my bad slim, this shit ain't for us! Slim I hear you go!" he said passing Vedo the blunt. "Vedo take this $50 and get us a box of blunts and a bottle of Moet, this is the least I can do, being though you just coming home and shit!"

Cruddy said with a disarming smile. If Vedo only knew Cruddy was setting him up. They say if the fish would not have bit the worm, he wouldn't got hooked. As soon as Vedo walked off, Cruddy flipped open his cell and punched in a number.

"Rell!" he barked through the phone. "Moe I'm on the basketball court and everything is everything!"

Rell had a plan on killing Vedo on his way back to Hope Village Halfway House. He didn't care where it happened, just as long as it happened. When Rell and his crew pulled up, Cruddy and Vedo was getting twisted. Cruddy spotted Rell and crew creeping toward them pulling their hoodies over their heads.

"Vedo....I'll be right back, I got to go take a piss!"

No fast as Cruddy walked off the trio rush over, guns drawn, fingers on their trigger, firing shots after shots with array of bullets, causing blood and skull to splatter everywhere, laying Vedo to rest. After it was all said and done, the trio walk off to the truck and pulled off without a care in the world.

ANOTHER MURDER IN THE MEAN DC STREET

Jamal was alone walking on pins and needles, in a cell at the DC jail. Ready to sing like a mocking bird. He was there doing what the other rat motherfucker do, jump on board with government, after getting arrested and being charged with conspiracy with distribution of marijuana, crack and methamphetamines, he was facing at least 20 years in prison. It's so crazy how niggas be talking I'm a man shit, before getting locked up, then turn around and be ready to snitch before a bitch. He would tell on their mother, woman even on their kids, for a measly time reduction. Jamal had plans on snitching on his crew in Atlanta, he never got a chance, them rat bastard beat him to it. He knew after snitching his life would never be the same. Coming from a family that would never condone or accept his action. He looked over at the shit that was hanging on his bunk. He started hearing sounds in his head.

"Do it... You rat piece of shit!"

"No!" he shouted putting his hands over his ears trying to block it out!" The sounds got louder and much clearer.

"Do it bitch...Do it!"

A small tear fell from his eyes, finally he built the nerve then grabbed the sheet, he tied it to the top bar of his cell. Making it into a rope, then took the rope and made a knot around his neck.

"Do it was the last sounds he heard, before leaping off his bunk to his death."

Nina had left the Florida Ave. market after giving Rell a book bag with $100,000.00 that she got from Bunny. She was headed to the Holiday Inn on New York Ave., with a $100 and a half ounce of rocks. She pulled up beside a 1985 Honda Accord with paper tags, then honked her horn twice the looked up at the window to room 112. She noticed the curtain open then shut. She grabbed her purse the hopped out, then hit her alarm. She looked around then walked up to the room. When the door opened, there stood the person she was there to meet, with sweat pouring out his pores. She walked in, it felt like a sauna, from all the smoke and heat in there.

"Thank you John!" she said passing him the money and drugs. She walked back out the same way she came in sashaying her ass to her car. Even though he was a crackhead, he still was a man, he watched her switching her ass. He didn't notice Rell sitting parked over in the corner, hunched low in his seat.

Prosecutor Phyllis Johnson was sitting at a table the La Fontaine Bleue Resort in Miami, wearing a flamingo pink Monique Lhuillier dress and a pair of Alexander Wang heels, and some Michael Kors sunglasses. She was wearing a 5 carat diamond

Vera Wang ring that could be seen from across the room, sipping on a cup of french vanilla cappuccino, waiting on the love of her life. A few seconds later he walked in with a dozen of red roses, he was in his late forties, if you hadn't known him you may have assumed he was in his thirties. He was very handsome, sensitive and a great listener, that's what she loved the most about him. If it wasn't for her job they would've gotten married.

"Hello beautiful." he spoke passing her the roses.

She had a brought smile on her face. "Are these for me?"

"Of course!"

The server walked up with a pen and pad. "Can I help you with something sir?"

"Yes can I have the irish cream cappuccino?"

"Sure I'll be right back in a second!"

Phyllis kissed him on his lips he enjoyed his wetness from her soft lips. He had plans on taking her on a cruise up the Florida Coast to propose. Her cell rang, destroying the moment, if it wasn't for her waiting for a call from her secretary she would have let go to voicemail.

"Hello... Un hun....alright thank you!" she hung up her cell with a bright smile on her face.

Tim was found not guilty for Rome's death. The charges for the shooting and murders on Orleans street were dropped. He was found guilty of possession of a firearm, and was sentenced to 60 months in the feds. Niecy changed her number, after putting the house up for sale, She packed up and moved away and had not been seen since. Curly sold the Stadium, he and Pat became back good friends. He and Pat agreed to go to Tom's grave site together every year on his birthday. Prosecutor Johnson resigned right after Tim's trial and moved to Tampa, Florida and opened up her own private law firm. She finally married the love of her life. She was now known as Mrs. Phyllis Johnson Cotton.

The End